BEWARE THE FULL MOON

■

ENGLISH WEREWOLVES IN FACT AND FICTION

Copyright © 2011 Read Books Ltd.
This book is copyright and may not be
reproduced or copied in any way without
the express permission of the publisher in writing

British Library Cataloguing-in-Publication Data
A catalogue record for this book is available from
the British Library

Contents

PAGE. NO

Gabriel-Ernest............ 1
SAKI

Hugues, the Wer-Wolf.. 10
SUTHERLAND MENZIES

The Terror in the Snow...........................33
B. FLETCHER ROBINSON

Reports in the British Isles............................52
MONTAGUE SUMMERS

Gabriel-Ernest

Saki

'There is a wild beast in your woods,' said the artist Cunningham, as he was being driven to the station. It was the only remark he had made during the drive, but as Van Cheele had talked incessantly his companion's silence had not been noticeable.

'A stray fox or two and some resident weasels. Nothing more formidable,' said Van Cheele. The artist said nothing.

'What did you mean about a wild beast?' said Van Cheele later, when they were on the platform.

'Nothing. My imagination. Here is the train,' said Cunningham.

That afternoon Van Cheele went for one of his frequent rambles through his woodland property. He had a stuffed bittern in his study, and knew the names of quite a number of wild flowers, so his aunt had possibly some justification in describing him as a great naturalist. At any rate, he was a great walker. It was his custom to take mental notes of everything he saw during his walks, not so much for the purpose of assisting contemporary science as to provide topics for conversation afterwards. When the bluebells began to show themselves in flower he made a point of informing everyone of the fact; the season of the year might have warned his hearers of the likelihood of such an occurrence, but at least they felt that he was being absolutely frank with them.

What Van Cheele saw on this particular afternoon was, however, something far removed from his ordinary range of experience. On a shelf of smooth stone overhanging a deep pool in the hollow of an oak coppice a boy of about sixteen lay asprawl, drying his wet brown limbs luxuriously in the sun. His wet hair, parted by a recent dive, lay close to his head, and his light-brown eyes, so light that there was an almost tigerish gleam in them, were turned towards Van Cheele with a certain lazy watchfulness. It was an unexpected apparition, and Van Cheele found himself engaged in the novel process of thinking before he spoke. Where on earth could this wild-looking boy hail from? The miller's wife had lost a child some two months ago, supposed to have been swept away by the mill-race, but that had been a mere baby, not a half-grown lad.

'What are you doing there?' he demanded.

'Obviously, sunning myself,' replied the boy.

'Where do you live?'

'Here, in these woods.'

'You can't live in the woods,' said Van Cheele.

'They are very nice woods,' said the boy, with a touch of patronage in his voice.

'But where do you sleep at night?'

'I don't sleep at night; that's my busiest time.'

Van Cheele began to have an irritated feeling that he was grappling with a problem that was eluding him.

'What do you feed on?' he asked.

'Flesh,' said the boy, and he pronounced the word with slow relish, as though he were tasting it.

'Flesh! What flesh?'

'Since it interests you, rabbits, wild-fowl, hares, poultry, lambs in their season, children when I can get any; they're usually too well locked in at night, when I do most of my hunting. It's quite two months since I tasted child-flesh.'

Ignoring the chaffing nature of the last remark, Van Cheele tried to draw the boy on the subject of possible poaching operations.

'You're talking rather through your hat when you speak of feeding on hares.' (Considering the nature of the boy's toilet, the smile was hardly an apt one.) 'Our hillside hares aren't easily caught.'

'At night I hunt on four feet,' was the somewhat cryptic response.

'I suppose you mean that you hunt with a dog?' hazarded Van Cheele.

The boy rolled slowly over on to his back, and laughed a weird low laugh, that was pleasantly like a chuckle and disagreeably like a snarl.

'I don't fancy any dog would be very anxious for my company, especially at night.'

Van Cheele began to feel that there was something positively uncanny about the strange-eyed, strange-tongued youngster.

'I can't have you staying in these woods,' he declared authoritatively.

'I fancy you'd rather have me here than in your house,' said the boy.

The prospect of this wild, nude animal in Van Cheele's primly ordered house was certainly an alarming one.

'If you don't go I shall have to make you,' said Van Cheele.

The boy turned like a flash, plunged into the pool, and in a moment had flung his wet and glistening body half-way up the bank where Van Cheele was standing. In an otter the movement would not have been remarkable; in a boy Van Cheele found it sufficiently startling. His foot slipped as he made an involuntary backward movement, and he found himself almost prostrate on the slippery weed-grown bank, with those tigerish yellow eyes not very far from his own. Almost instinctively he half-raised his hand to his throat. The boy laughed again, a laugh in which the snarl had nearly driven out the chuckle, and then, with another of his astonishing lightning movements, plunged out of view into a yielding tangle of weed and fern.

'What an extraordinary wild animal!' said Van Cheele as he picked himself up. And then he recalled Cunningham's remark, 'There is a wild beast in your woods.'

Walking slowly homeward, Van Cheele began to turn over in his mind various local occurrences which might be traceable to the existence of this astonishing young savage.

Something had been thinning the game in the woods lately, poultry had been missing from the farms, hares were growing unaccountably scarcer, and complaints had reached him of lambs being carried off bodily from the hills. Was it possible that this wild boy was really hunting the countryside in company with some clever poacher dog? He had spoken of hunting 'four-footed' by night, but then, again, he had hinted strangely at no dog caring to come near him, 'especially at night'. It was certainly puzzling. And then, as Van Cheele ran his mind over the various depredations that had been committed during the last month or two, he came suddenly to a dead stop, alike in his walk and his speculations. The child missing from the mill two months ago – the accepted theory was that it had tumbled into the mill race and been swept away; but the mother had always declared she had heard a shriek on the hill side of the house, in the opposite direction from the water. It was unthinkable, of course, but he wished that the boy had not made that uncanny remark about child-flesh eaten two months ago. Such dreadful things should not be said even in fun.

Van Cheele, contrary to his usual wont, did not feel disposed to be communicative about his discovery in the wood. His position as a parish councillor and justice of the peace seemed somehow compromised by the fact that he was harbouring a personality of such doubtful repute on his property; there was even a possibility that a heavy bill of damages for raided lambs and poultry might be laid at his door. At dinner that night he was quite unusually silent.

'Where's your voice gone to?' said his aunt. 'One would think you had seen a wolf.'

Van Cheele, who was not familiar with the old saying, thought the remark rather foolish; if he *had* seen a wolf on his property his tongue would have been extraordinarily busy with the subject.

At breakfast next morning Van Cheele was conscious that his feeling of uneasiness regarding yesterday's episode had not wholly disappeared, and he resolved to go by train to the neighbouring cathedral town, hunt up Cunningham, and learn from him what he had really seen that had prompted the remark about a wild beast in the woods. With this resolution taken, his usual cheerfulness partially returned, and he hummed a bright little melody as he sauntered to the morning-room for his customary cigarette. As he entered the room the melody made way abruptly for a pious invocation. Gracefully asprawl on the ottoman, in an attitude of almost exaggerated repose, was the boy of the woods. He was drier than when Van Cheele had last seen him, but no other alteration was noticeable in his toilet.

'How dare you come here?' asked Van Cheele furiously.

'You told me I was not to stay in the woods,' said the boy calmly.

'But not to come here. Supposing my aunt should see you!'

And with a view to minimising that catastrophe Van Cheele hastily obscured as much of his unwelcome guest as possible under the folds of a *Morning Post*. At that moment his aunt entered the room.

'This is a poor boy who has lost his way – and lost his memory. He doesn't know who he is or where he comes from,' explained Van Cheele desperately, glancing apprehensively at the waif's face to see whether he was going to add inconvenient candour to his other savage propensities.

Miss Van Cheele was enormously interested.

'Perhaps his underlinen is marked,' she suggested.

'He seems to have lost most of that, too,' said Van Cheele, making frantic little grabs at the *Morning Post* to keep it in its place.

A naked homeless child appealed to Miss Van Cheele as warmly as a stray kitten or derelict puppy would have done.

'We must do all we can for him,' she decided, and in a very short time a messenger, dispatched to the rectory, where a page-boy was kept, had returned with a suit of pantry clothes, and the necessary accessories of shirt, shoes, collar, etc. Clothed, clean, and groomed, the boy lost none of his uncanniness in Van Cheele's eyes, but his aunt found him sweet.

'We must call him something till we know who he really is,' she said. 'Gabriel-Ernest, I think; those are nice suitable names.'

Van Cheele agreed, but he privately doubted whether they were being grafted on to a nice suitable child. His misgivings were not diminished by the fact that his staid and elderly spaniel had bolted out of the house at the first incoming of the boy, and now obstinately remained shivering and yapping at the farther end of the orchard, while the canary, usually as vocally industrious as Van Cheele himself, had put itself on an allowance of frightened cheeps. More than ever he was resolved to consult Cunningham without loss of time.

As he drove off to the station his aunt was arranging that Gabriel-Ernest should help her to entertain the infant members of her Sunday-school class at tea that afternoon.

Cunningham was not at first disposed to be communicative.

'My mother died of some brain trouble,' he explained, 'so you will understand why I am averse to dwelling on anything of an impossibly fantastic nature that I may see or think that I have seen.'

'But what *did* you see?' persisted Van Cheele.

'What I thought I saw was something so extraordinary that no really sane man could dignify it with the credit of having actually happened. I was standing, the last evening I was with you, half-hidden in the hedgegrowth by the orchard gate, watching the dying glow of the sunset. Suddenly I became aware of a naked boy, a bather from some neighbouring pool, I took him to be, who was standing out on the bare hillside also watching the sunset. His pose was so suggestive of some wild faun of Pagan myth that I instantly wanted to engage him as a model, and in another moment I think I should have hailed him. But just then the sun dipped out of view, and all the orange and pink slid of the landscape, leaving it cold and grey. And at the same moment an astounding thing happened – the boy vanished too!'

'What! vanished away into nothing?' asked Van Cheele excitedly.

'No; that is the dreadful part of it,' answered the artist; 'on the open hillside where the boy had been standing a second ago, stood a large wolf, blackish in colour, with gleaming fangs and cruel, yellow eyes. You may think—'

But Van Cheele did not stop for anything as futile as thought.

Already he was tearing at top speed towards the station. He dismissed the idea of a telegram. 'Gabriel-Ernest is a werewolf' was a hopelessly inadequate effort at conveying the situation, and his aunt would think it was a code message to which he had omitted to give her the key. His one hope was that he might reach home before sundown. The cab which he chartered at the other end of the railway journey bore him with what seemed exasperating slowness along the country roads, which were pink and mauve with the flush of the sinking sun. His aunt was putting away some unfinished jams and cake when he arrived.

'Where is Gabriel-Ernest?' he almost screamed.

'He is taking the little Toop child home,' said his aunt. 'It was getting so late, I thought it wasn't safe to let it go back alone. What a lovely sunset, isn't it?'

But Van Cheele, although not oblivious of the glow in the western sky, did not stay to discuss its beauties. At a speed for which he was scarcely geared he raced along the narrow lane that led to the home of the Toops. On one side ran the swift current of the mill-stream, on the other rise the stretch of bare hillside. A dwindling rim of red sun showed still on the skyline, and the next turning must bring him in view of the ill-assorted couple he was pursuing. Then the colour went suddenly out of things, and a grey light settled itself with a quick shiver over the landscape. Van Cheele heard a shrill wail of fear, and stopped running.

Nothing was ever seen again of the Toop child or Gabriel-Ernest, but the latter's discarded garments were found lying in the road, so it was assumed that the child had fallen into the water, and that the boy had stripped and jumped in, in a vain endeavour to save it. Van Cheele and some workmen who were near by at the time testified to having heard a child scream loudly just near the spot where the clothes were found. Mrs Toop, who had eleven other children, was decently resigned to her bereavement, but Miss Van Cheele sincerely mourned her lost foundling. It was on her initiative that a memorial brass was put up in the parish church to 'Gabriel-Ernest, an unknown boy, who bravely sacrificed his life for another.'

Van Cheele gave way to his aunt in most things, but he flatly refused to subscribe to the Gabriel-Ernest memorial.

Hugues, the Wer-Wolf

I

On the confines of that extensive forest-tract formerly spreading over so large a portion of the county of Kent, a remnant of which, to this day, is known as the weald* of Kent, and where it stretched its almost impervious covert midway between Ashford and Canterbury during the prolonged reign of our second Henry, a family of Norman extraction by name Hugues (or Wulfric, as they were commonly called by the Saxon inhabitants of that district) had, under protection of the ancient forest laws, furtively erected for themselves a lone and miserable habitation. And amidst those sylvan fastnesses, ostensibly following the occupation of woodcutters, the wretched outcasts, for such, from some cause or other, they evidently were, had for many years maintained a secluded and precarious existence. Whether from the rooted antipathy still actively cherished against all of that usurping nation from which they derived their origin, or from recorded malpractice by their superstitious Anglo-Saxon neighbours, they had long been looked upon as belonging to the accursed race of wer-wolves, and as such churlishly refused

* That woody district, at the period to which our tale belongs, was an immense forest, desolate of inhabitants, and only occupied by wild swine and deer; and though it is now filled with towns and villages and well peopled, the woods that remain sufficiently indicate its former extent.

work on the domains of the surrounding franklins or proprietors, so thoroughly was accredited the descent of the original lycanthropic stain transmitted from father to son through several generations. That the Hugues Wulfric reckoned not a single friend among the adjacent homesteads of serf or freedman was not to be wondered at, possessing as they did so unenviable a reputation; for to them was invariably attributed even the misfortunes which chance alone might seem to have given birth. Did midnight fire consume the grange; – did the time-decayed barn, over-stored with an abundant harvest, tumble into ruins; – were the shocks of wheat lain prostrate over the fields by a tempest; – did the smut destroy the grain; – or the cattle perish, decimated by a murrain; – a child sink under some wasting malady; – or a woman give premature birth to her offspring, it was ever the Hugues Wulfric who were openly accused, eyed askance with mingled fear and detestation, the finger of young and old pointing them out with bitter execrations – in fine, they were almost as nearly classed *feroe natura* as their fabled prototype, and dealt with accordingly.*

Terrible, indeed, were the tales told of them round the glowing hearth at eventide, whilst spinning the flax, or plucking the geese; equally affirmed too, in broad daylight, whilst driving the cows to pasturage, and most circumstantially discussed on Sundays between mass and vespers, by the gossip groups collected within Ashford parvyse, with most seasonable admixture of anathema and devout crossings. Witchcraft, larceny, murther, and sacrilege, formed prominent features in the bloody and mysterious scenes of which the Hugues Wulfric were the alleged actors: sometimes they were ascribed to the father, at others to the mother, and even the sister escaped not her share of vilification; fain would they have attributed an

*King Edgar is said to have been the first who attempted to rid England of these animals; criminals even being pardoned by producing a stated number of these creatures' tongues. Some centuries after they increased to such a degree as to become again the object of royal attention; and Edward I appointed persons to extirpate this obnoxious race. It is one of the principal bearings in armoury. Hugh, surnamed *Lupus*, the first Earl of Kent, bore for his crest a wolf's head.

atrocious disposition to the unweaned babe, so great, so universal was the horror in which they held that race of Cain! The churchyard at Ashford, and the stone cross, from whence diverged the several roads to London, Canterbury, and Ashford situated midway between the two latter places, served, so tradition avouched, as nocturnal theatres for the unhallowed deeds of the Wulfrics, who thither prowled by moonlight, it was said to batten on the freshly-buried dead, or drain the blood of any living wight who might be rash enough to venture among those solitary spots. True it was that the wolves had, during some of the severe winters, emerged from their forest lairs, and entering the cemetery by a breach in its walls, goaded by famine, had actually disinterred the dead; true was it, also, that the Wolf's Cross, as the hinds commonly designated it, had been stained with gore on one occasion through the fall of a drunken mendicant, who chanced to fracture his skull against a pointed angle of its basement. But these accidents, as well as a multitude of others, were attributed to the guilty intervention of the Wulfrics, under their fiendish guise of wer-wolves.

These poor people, moreover, took no pains to justify themselves from a prejudice so monstrous: full well apprised of what calumny they were the victims, but alike conscious of their impotence to contradict it, they tacitly suffered its infliction, and fled all contact with those to whom they knew themselves repulsive. Shunning the highways, and never venturing to pass through the town of Ashford in open day, they pursued such labour as might occupy them within doors, or in unfrequented places. They appeared not at Canterbury market, never numbered themselves amongst the pilgrims at Becket's far-famed shrine, or assisted at any sport, merry-making, haycutting, or harvest home: the priest had interdicted them from all communion with the church – the ale-bibbers from the hostelry.

The primitive cabin which they inhabited was built of chalk and clay, with a thatch of straw, in which the high winds had made huge rents and closed up by a rotten door, exhibiting wide gaps, through which the gusts had free ingress. As this

Hugues, the Wer-Wolf

wretched abode was situated at considerable distance from any other, if, perchance, any of the neighbouring serfs strayed within its precincts towards nightfall, their credulous fears made them shun near approach so soon as the vapours of the marsh were seen to blend their ghastly wreaths with the twilight; and as that darkling time drew on which explains the diabolical sense of the old saying, ''tween dog and wolf,' ''twixt hawk and buzzard,' at that hour the will-o'-wisps began to glimmer around the dwelling of the Wulfrics, who patriarchally supped – whenever they had a supper – and forthwith betook themselves to their rest.

Sorrow, misery, and the putrid exhalations of the steeped hemp, from which they manufactured a rude and scanty attire, combined eventually to bring sickness and death into the bosom of this wretched family, who, in their utmost extremity, could neither hope for pity or succour. The father was first attacked, and his corpse was scarce cold ere the mother rendered up her breath. Thus passed that fated couple to their account, unsolaced by the consolation of the confessor, or the medicaments of the leech. Hugues Wulfric, their eldest son, himself dug their grave, laid their bodies within it swathed with hempen shreds for grave cloths, and raised a few clods of earth to mark their last resting-place. A hind, who chanced to see him fulfilling this pious duty in the dusk of evening, crossed himself, and fled as fast as his legs would carry him, fully believing that he had assisted at some hellish incantation. When the real event transpired, the neighbouring gossips congratulated one another upon the double mortality, which they looked upon as the tardy chastisement of heaven: they spoke of ringing the bells, and singing masses of thanks for such an action of grace.

It was All Souls' eve, and the wind howled along the bleak hillside, whistling drearily through the naked branches of the forest trees, whose last leaves it had long since stripped; the sun had disappeared; a dense and chilling fog spread through the air like the mourning veil of the widowed, whose day of love hath early fled. No star shone in the still and murky sky. In that

Hugues, the Wer-Wolf

lonely hut, through which death had so lately passed, the orphan survivors held their lonely vigil by the fitful blaze emitted by the reeking logs upon their hearth. Several days had elapsed since their lips had been imprinted for the last time upon the cold hands of their parents; several dreary nights had passed since the sad hour in which their eternal farewell had left them desolate on earth.

Poor lone ones! Both, too, in the flower of their youth – how sad, yet how serene did they appear amid their grief! But what sudden and mysterious terror is it that seems to overcome them? It is not, alas! the first time since they were left alone upon earth that they have found themselves at this hour of the night by their deserted hearth, enlivened of old by the cheerful tales of their mother. Full often had they wept together over her memory, but never yet had their solitude proved so appalling; and, pallid as very spectres, they tremblingly gazed upon one another as the flickering ray from the wood-fire played over their features.

'Brother! heard you not that loud shriek which every echo of the forest repeated? It sounds to me as if the ground were ringing with the tread of some gigantic phantom, and whose breath seems to have shaken the door of our hut. The breath of the dead they say is icy cold. A mortal shivering has come over me.'

'And I, too, sister, thought I heard voices as it were at a distance, murmuring strange words. Tremble not thus – am I not beside you?'

'Oh, brother! let us pray the Holy Virgin, to the end that she may restrain the departed from haunting our dwelling.'

'But, perhaps, our mother is amongst them: she comes, unshrived and unshrouded, to visit her forlorn offspring – her well-beloved! For, knowest thou not, sister, 'tis the eve on which the dead forsake their tombs. Let us open the door, that our mother may enter and resume her wonted place by the hearthstone.'

'Oh, brother, how gloomy is all without doors, how damp and cold the gust sweeps by. Hearest thou, what groans the dead are uttering round our hut? Oh, close the door, in heaven's name!'.

'Take courage, sister, I have thrown upon the fire that holy branch, plucked as it flowered on last Palm Sunday, which thou knowest will drive away all evil spirits, and now our mother can enter alone.'

'But how will she look, brother? They say the dead are horrible to gaze upon; that their hair has fallen away; their eyes become hollow; and that, in walking, their bones rattle hideously. Will our mother, then, be thus?'.

'No; she will appear with the features we loved to behold; with the affectionate smile that welcomed us home from our perilous labours; with the voice which, in early youth, sought us when, belated, the closing night surprised us far from our dwelling.'

The poor girl busied herself awhile in arranging a few platters of scanty fare upon the tottering board which served them for a table; and this last pious offering of filial love, as she deemed it, appeared accomplished only by the greatest and last effort, so enfeebled had her frame become.

'Let our dearly-beloved mother enter then,' she exclaimed, sinking exhausted upon the settle. 'I have prepared her evening meal, that she may not be angry with me, and all is arranged as she was wont to have it. But what ails thee, my brother, for now thou tremblest as I did awhile agone?'

'See'st thou not, sister, those pale lights which are rising at a distance across the marsh? They are the dead, coming to seat themselves before the repast prepared for them. Hark! list to the funeral tones of the Allhallowtide* bells, as they come upon the gale, blended with their hollow voices. – Listen, listen!'

'Brother, this horror grows insupportable. This, I feel, of a verity, will be my last night upon earth! And is there no word of hope to cheer me, mingling with those fearful sounds? Oh, mother! mother!'

'Hush, sister, hush! see'st thou now the ghastly lights which

*On this eve formally the Catholic church performed a most solemn office for the repose of the dead.

herald the dead, gleaming athwart the horizon? Hearest thou the prolonged tolling of the bell? They come! they come!'
'Eternal repose to their ashes!' exclaimed the bereaved ones, sinking upon their knees, and bowing down their heads in the extremity of terror and lamentation; and as they uttered the words, the door was at the same moment closed with violence, as though it had been slammed to by a vigorous hand. Hugues started to his feet, for the cracking of the timber which supported the roof seemed to announce the fall of the frail tenement; the fire was suddenly extinguished, and a plaintive groan mingled itself with the blast that whistled through the crevices of the door. On raising his sister, Hugues found that she too was no longer to be numbered among the living.

II

Hugues, on becoming the head of his family, composed of two sisters younger than himself, saw them likewise descend into the grave in the short space of a fortnight; and when he had laid the last within her parent earth, he hesitated whether he should not extend himself beside them, and share their peaceful slumber. It was not by tears and sobs that grief so profound as his manifested itself, but in a mute and sullen contemplation over the supulture of his kindred and his own future happiness. During three consecutive nights he wandered, pale and haggard, from his solitary hut, to prostrate himself and kneel by turns upon the funereal turf. For three days food had not passed his lips.

Winter had interrupted the labours of the woods and fields, and Hugues had presented himself in vain among the neighbouring domains to obtain a few days' employment to thresh grain, cut wood, or drive the plough; no one would employ him from fear of drawing upon himself the fallity attached to all bearing the name of Wulfric. He met with brutal denials at all hands, and not only were these accompanied by taunts and menace, but dogs were let loose upon him to rend his limbs; they deprived him even of the alms accorded to beggars by profession; in short, he found himself overwhelmed with injuries and scorn.

Was he, then, to expire of inanition or deliver himself from the tortures of hunger by suicide? He would have embraced that means, as a last and only consolation, had he not been retained earthward to struggle with his dark fate by a feeling of love. Yes, that abject being, forced in very desperation, against his better self, to abhor the human species in the abstract, and to feel a savage joy in waging war against it; that *paria* who scarce longer felt confidence in that heaven which seemed an apathetic witness of his woes; that man so isolated from those social relations which alone compensate us for the toils and troubles of life, without other stay than that afforded by his conscience, with no other fortune in prospect than the bitter existence and miserable death of his departed kin: worn to the bone by privation and sorrow, swelling with rage and resentment, he yet consented to live – to cling to life; for, strange – he loved! But for that heaven-sent ray gleaming across his thorny path, a pilgrimage so lone and wearisome would he have gladly exchanged for the peaceful slumber of the grave.

Hugues Wulfric would have been the finest youth in all that part of Kent, were it not that the outrages with which he had so unceasingly to contend, and the privations he was forced to undergo, had effaced the colour from his cheeks, and sunk his eyes deep in their orbits: his brows were habitually contracted, and his glance oblique and fierce. Yet, despite that recklessness and anguish which clouded his features, one, incredulous of his atrocities, could not have failed to admire the savage beauty of his head, cast in nature's noblest mould, crowned with a profusion of waving hair, and set upon shoulders whose robust and harmonious proportions were discoverable through the tattered attire investing them. His carriage was firm and majestic; his motions were not without a species of rustic grace, and the tone of his naturally soft voice accorded admirably with the purity in which he spoke his ancestral language – the Norman-French: in short, he differed so widely from people of his imputed condition that one is constrained to believe that jealousy

Hugues, the Wer-Wolf

or prejudice must originally have been no stranger to the malicious persecution of which he was the object. The women alone ventured first to pity his forlorn condition, and endeavoured to think of him in a more favourable light.

Branda, niece of Willieblud, the flesher of Ashford, had, among other of the town maidens, noticed Hugues with a not unfavouring eye, as she chanced to pass one day on horseback, through a coppice near the outskirts of the town, into which the latter had been led by the eager chase of a wild hog, and which animal, from the nature of the country was, single-handed, exceedingly difficult of capture. The malignant falsehoods of the ancient crones, continually buzzed in her ears, in nowise diminished the advantageous opinion she had conceived of this ill-treated and good-looking wer-wolf. She sometimes, indeed, went so far as to turn considerably out of her way, in order to meet and exchange his cordial greeting: for Hugues, recognizing the attention of which he had now become the object, had, in his turn, at last summoned up courage to survey more leisurely the pretty Branda; and the result was that he found her as buxom and pretty a lass as, in his hitherto restricted rambles out of the forest, his timorous gaze had ever encountered. His gratitude increased proportionally; and at the moment when his domestic losses came one after another to overwhelm him, he was actually on the eve of making Branda, on the first opportunity presenting itself, an avowal of the love he bore her.

It was chill winter – Christmas-tide – the distant roll of the curfew had long ceased, and all the inhabitants of Ashford were safe housed in their tenements for the night. Hugues, solitary, motionless, silent, his forehead grasped between his hands, his gaze dully fixed upon the decaying brands that feebly glimmered upon his hearth: he heeded not the cutting north wind, whose sweeping gusts shook the crazy roof, and whistled through the chinks of the door; he started not at the harsh cries of the herons fighting for prey in the marsh, nor at the dismal croaking of the ravens perched over his smoke-vent. He thought of his departed kindred, and imagined that his hour to join them would soon be at hand; for the intense cold congealed the marrow of his bones, and fell hunger gnawed and twisted his entrails. Yet, at intervals, would a recollection of nascent love, of Branda, suddenly appease his else intolerable anguish, and cause a faint smile to gleam across his wan features.

'Oh, blessed Virgin! grant that my sufferings may speedily cease!' murmured he, despairingly. 'Oh, would I might be a wer-wolf, as they call me! I could then requite them for all the foul wrong done me. True, I could not nourish myself with their flesh; I would not shed their blood; but I would be able to terrify and torment those who have wrought my parents' and sisters' death – who have persecuted our family even to extermination! Why have I not the power to change my nature into that of a wolf, if, of a verity, my ancestors possessed it, as they avouch? I should at least find carrion to devour,* and not die thus horribly. Branda is the sole being in this world who cares for me; and that conviction alone reconciles me to life!'

Hugues gave free current to these gloomy reflections. The smouldering embers now emitted but a feeble and vacillating light, faintly struggling with the surrounding gloom, and Hugues felt the horror of darkness coming strong upon him; frozen with the ague-fit one instant, and troubled the next by the hurried pulsation of his veins, he arose, at last, to seek some fuel, and threw upon the fire a heap of faggot-chips, heath and straw, which soon raised a clear and crackling flame. His stock of wood had become exhausted, and, seeking wherewith to replenish his dying hearth-light, whilst foraging under the rude oven amongst a pile of rubbish placed there by his mother wherewith to bake bread – handles of tools, fractured joint-stools, and cracked platters, he discovered a chest rudely covered with a dressed hide, and which he had never seen before; and seizing upon it as though he had discovered a treasure, broke open the lid, strongly secured by a string.

This chest, which had evidently remained long unopened,

*Horseflesh was an article of food among our Saxon forefathers in England.

Hugues, the Wer-Wolf

contained the complete disguise of a wer-wolf: — a dyed sheepskin, with gloves in the form of paws, a tail, a mask with an elongated muzzle, and furnished with formidable rows of yellow horse-teeth.

Hugues started backwards, terrified at his discovery — so opportune, that it seemed to him the work of sorcery; then, on recovering from his surprise, he drew forth one by one the several pieces of this strange envelope, which had evidently seen some service, and from long neglect had become somewhat damaged. Then rushed confusedly upon his mind the marvellous recitals made him by his grandfather, as he nursed him upon his knees during earliest childhood; tales, during the narration of which his mother wept silently, as he laughed heartily. In his mind there was a mingled strife of feelings and purposes alike undefinable. He continued his silent examination of this criminal heritage, and by degrees his imagination grew bewildered with vague and extravagant projects.

Hunger and despair conjointly hurried him away: he saw objects no longer save through a bloody prism: he felt his very teeth on edge with an avidity for biting; he experienced an inconceivable desire to run: he set himself to howl as though he had practised wer-wolfery all his life, and began thoroughly to invest himself with the guise and attributes of his novel vocation. A more startling change could scarcely have been wrought in him, had that so horribly grotesque metamorphosis really been the effect of enchantment; aided, too, as it was, by the fever which generated a temporary insanity in his frenzied brain.

Scarcely did he thus find himself travestied into a wer-wolf through the influence of his vestment, ere he darted forth from th: hut, through the forest and into the open country, white with hoar frost, and across which the bitter north wind swept, howling in a frightful manner and traversing the meadows, fallows, plains, and marshes, like a shadow. But, at that hour, and during such a season, not a single belated wayfarer was there to encounter Hugues, whom the sharpness of the air, and the excitation of his course, had worked up to the highest pitch

Hugues, the Wer-Wolf

of extravagance and audacity: he howled the louder proportionally as his hunger increased.

Suddenly the heavy rumbling of an approaching vehicle arrested his attention; at first with indecision, then with a stupid fixity, he struggled with two suggestions, counselling him at one and the same time to fly and to advance. The carriage, or whatever it might be, continued, rolling towards him; the night was not so obscure but that he was enabled to distinguish the tower of Ashford church at a short distance off, and hard by which stood a pile of unhewn stone, destined either for the execution of some repair, or addition to the saintly edifice, in the shade of which he ran to crouch himself down, and so await the arrival of his prey.

It proved to be the covered cart of Willieblud, the Ashford flesher, who was wont twice a week to carry meat to Canterbury, and travelled by night in order that he might be among the first at market-opening. Of this Hugues was fully aware, and the departure of the flesher naturally suggested to him the inference that his niece must be keeping house by herself, for our lusty flesher had been long a widower. For an instant he hesitated whether he should introduce himself there, so favourable an opportunity thus presenting itself, or whether he should attack the uncle and seize upon his viands. Hunger got the better of love this once, and the monotonous whistle with which the driver was accustomed to urge forward his sorry jade warning him to be in readiness, he howled in a plaintive tone, and, rushing forward, seized the horse by the bit.

'Willieblud, flesher,' said he, disguising his voice, and speaking to him in the *lingua Franca* of that period, 'I hunger; throw me two pounds of meat if thou would'st have me live.'

'St Willifred have mercy on me!' cried the terrified flesher, 'is it thou, Hugues Wulfric, of Wealdmarsh, the born werwolf?'

'Thou say'st sooth – it is I,' replied Hugues, who had sufficient address to avail himself of the credulous superstition of Willieblud; 'I would rather have raw meat than eat of thy flesh, plump as thou art. Throw me, therefore, what I crave, and for-

Hugues, the Wer-Wolf

get not to be ready with the like portion each time thou settest out for Canterbury market; or, failing thereof, I tear thee limb from limb.'

Hugues, to display his attributes of a wer-wolf before the gaze of the confounded flesher, had mounted himself upon the spokes of the wheel, and placed his forepaw upon the edge of the cart, which he made semblance of snuffing at with his snout. Willieblud, who believed in wer-wolves as devoutly as he did in his patron saint, had no sooner perceived this monstrous paw, than, uttering a fervent invocation to the latter, he seized upon his daintiest joint of meat, let it fall to the ground, and whilst Hugues sprung eagerly down to pick it up, the butcher at the same instant having bestowed a sudden and violent blow upon the flank of his beast, the latter set off at a round gallop without waiting for any reiterated invitation from the lash.

Hugues was so satisfied with a repast which had cost him far less trouble to procure than any he had long remembered, readily promised himself the renewal of an expedient, the execution of which was at once easy and diverting; for though smitten with the charms of the fair-haired Branda, he not the less found a malicious pleasure in augmenting the terror of her uncle Willieblud. The latter, for a long while, revealed not to living being the tale of his terrible encounter and strange compact, which had varied according to circumstances, and he submitted unmurmuringly to the imposts levied each time the wer-wolf presented himself before him, without being very nice about either the weight or quality of the meat; he no longer even waited to be asked for it, anything to avoid the sight of that fiend-like form clinging to the side of his cart, or being brought into such immediate contact with that hideous misshapen paw stretched forth, as it were to strangle him, that paw too, which had once been a human hand. He had become dull and thoughtful of late; he set out to market unwillingly, and seemed to dread the hour of departure as it approached, and no longer beguiled the tedium of his nocturnal journey by whistling to his horse, or trolling snatches of ballads, as was his

Hugues, the Wer-Wolf

wont formerly; he now invariably returned in a melancholy and restless mood.

Branda, at loss to conceive what had given birth to this new and permanent depression which had taken possession of her uncle's mind, after in vain exhausting conjecture, proceeded to interrogate, importune, and supplicate him by turns, until the unhappy flesher, no longer proof against such continued appeals, at last disburthened himself of the load which he had at heart, by recounting the history of his adventure with the werwolf.

Branda listened to the whole of the recital without offering interruption or comment; but, at its close —

'Hugues is no more a wer-wolf than thou or I,' exclaimed she, offended that such unjust suspicion should be cherished against one for whom she had long felt more than an interest; ''tis an idle tale, or some juggling device; I fear me thou must needs dream these sorceries, uncle Willieblud, for Hugues of the Wealmarsh, or Wulfric, as the silly fools call him, is worth far more, I trow, than his reputation.'

'Girl, it boots not saying me nay, in this matter,' replied Willieblud, pertinaciously urging the truth of his story; 'the family of Hugues, as everybody knows, were wer-wolves born, and, since they are all of late, by the blessing of heaven, defunct, save one, Hugues now inherits the wolf's paw.'

'I tell thee, and will avouch it openly, uncle, that Hugues is of too gentle and seemly a nature to serve Satan, and turn himself into a wild beast, and that will I never believe until I have seen the like.'

'Mass, and that thou shalt right speedily, if thou wilt but along with me. In very troth 'tis he, besides, he made confession of his name, and did I not recognize his voice, and am I not ever bethinking me of his knavish paw, which he places me on the shaft while he stays the horse. Girl, he is in league with the foul fiend.'

Branda had, to a certain degree, imbibed the superstition in the abstract, equally with her uncle, and, excepting so far as it touched the hitherto, as she believed, traduced being on whom

Hugues, the Wer-Wolf

her affections, as if in feminine perversity, had so strangely lighted. Her woman's curiosity, in this instance, less determined her resolution to accompany the flesher on his next journey, than the desire to exculpate her lover, fully believing the strange tale of her kinsman's encounter with, and spoliation by the latter, to be the effect of some illusion, and of which to find him guilty, was the sole fear she experienced on mounting the rude vehicle laden with its ensanguined viands.

It was just midnight when they started from Ashford, the hour alike dear to wer-wolves as to spectres of every denomination. Hugues was punctual at the appointed spot; his howlings, as they drew nigh, though horrible enough, had still something human in them, and disconcerted not a little the doubts of Branda. Willieblud, however, trembled even more than she did, and sought for the wolf's portion; the latter raised himself upon his hind legs, and extended one of his forepaws to receive his pittance as soon as the cart stopped at the heap of stones.

'Uncle, I shall swoon with affright,' exclaimed Branda, clinging closely to the flesher, and tremblingly pulling the coverchief over her eyes: 'loose rein and smite thy beast, or evil will surely betide us.'

'Thou are not alone, gossip,' cried Hugues, fearful of a snare; 'if thou essay'st to play me false, thou art at once undone.'

'Harm us not friend Hugues, thou know'st I weigh not my pounds of meat with thee; I shall take care to keep my troth. It is Branda, my niece, who goes with me tonight to buy wares at Canterbury.'

'Branda with thee? By the mass 'tis she indeed, more buxom and rosy too, than ever; come pretty one, descend and tarry awhile, that I may have speech with thee.'

'I conjure thee, good Hugues, terrify not so cruelly my poor wench, who is wellnigh dead already with fear; suffer us to hold our way, for we have far to go, and the morrow is early market-day.'

'Go thy ways then alone, uncle Willieblud, 'tis thy niece I

Hugues, the Wer-Wolf

would have speech with, in all courtesy and honour; the which, if thou permittest not readily, and of a good grace, I will rend thee both to death.'

All in vain was it that Willieblud exhausted himself in prayers and lamentations in hopes of softening the bloodthirsty wer-wolf, as he believed him to be, refusing as the latter did, every sort of compromise in avoidance of his demand, and at last replying only by horrible threats, which froze the hearts of both. Branda, although especially interested in the debate, neither stirred foot, or opened her mouth, so greatly had terror and surprise overwhelmed her; she kept her eyes fixed upon the wolf, who peered at her likewise through his mask, and felt incapable of offering resistance when she found herself forcibly dragged out of the vehicle, and deposited by an invisible power, as it seemed to her, beside the piles of stones; she swooned without uttering a single scream.

The flesher was no less dumbfounded at the turn which the adventure had taken, and he, too, fell back among his meat as though stricken by a blinding blow; he fancied that the wolf had swept his bushy tail violently across his eyes, and on recovering the use of his senses found himself alone in the cart, which rolled joltingly at a swift pace towards Canterbury. At first he listened, but in vain, for the wind bringing him either the shrieks of his niece, or the howlings of the wolf; but stop his beast he could not, which, panic-stricken, kept trotting as though bewitched, or felt the spur of some fiend pricking her flanks.

Willieblud, however, reached his journey's end in safety, sold his meat, and returned to Ashford, reckoning full sure upon having to say a *De Profundis* for his niece, whose fate he had not ceased to bemoan during the whole night. But how great was his astonishment to find her safe at home, a little pale, from recent fright and want of sleep, but without a scratch; still more was he astonished to hear that the wolf had done her no injury whatsoever, contenting himself, after she had recovered from her swoon, with conducting her back to their dwelling, and acting in every respect like a loyal suitor, rather than a sanguinary wer-wolf. Willieblud knew not what to think of it.

This nocturnal gallantry towards his niece had additionally irritated the burly Saxon against the wer-wolf, and although the fear of reprisals kept him from making a direct and public attack upon Hugues, he ruminated not the less upon taking some sure and secret revenge; but previous to putting his design into execution, it struck him that he could not do better than relate his misadventures to the ancient sacristan and parish grave-digger of St Michael's, a worthy of profound sagacity in those sort of matters, endowed with a clerk-like erudition, and consulted as an oracle by all the old crones and lovelorn maidens throughout the township of Ashford and its vicinity.

'Slay a wer-wolf thou canst not,' was the repeated rejoinder of the wiseacre to the earnest queries of the tormented flesher; 'for his hide is proof against spear or arrow, though vulnerable to the edge of a cutting weapon of steel. I counsel thee to deal him a slight flesh wound, or cut him over the paw, in order to know of a surety whether it really be Hugues or no; thou'lt run no danger, save thou strikest him a blow from which blood flows not therefrom, for, so soon as his skin is severed he taketh flight.'

Resolving implicitly to follow the advice of the sacristan, Willieblud that same evening determined to know with what wer-wolf it was with whom he had to do, and with that view hid his cleaver, newly sharpened for the occasion, under the load in his cart, and resolutely prepared to make use of it as a preparatory step towards proving the identity of Hugues with the audacious spoiler of his meat, and eke his peace. The wolf presented himself as usual, and anxiously inquired after Branda, which stimulated the flesher the more firmly to follow out his design.

'Here, Wolf,' said Willieblud, stooping down as if to choose a piece of meat; 'I give thee double portion tonight; up with thy paw, take toll, and be mindful of my frank alms.'

'Sooth, I will remember me, gossip,' rejoined our wer-wolf;

'but when shall the marriage be solemnized for certain, betwixt the fair Branda and myself?'

Hugues believing he had nothing to fear from the flesher, whose meats he so readily appropriated to himself, and of whose fair niece he hoped shortly no less to make lawful possession; both that he really loved, and viewed his union with her as the surest means of placing him within the pale of that sociality from which he had been so unjustly exiled, could he but succeed in making intercession with the holy fathers of the church to remove their interdict. Hugues placed his extended paw upon the edge of the cart; but instead of handing him his joint of beef, or mutton, Willieblud raised his cleaver, and at a single blow lopped off the paw laid there as fittingly for the purpose as though upon a block. The flesher flung down his weapon, and belaboured his beast, the wer-wolf roared aloud with agony, and disappeared amid the dark shades of the forest, in which, aided by the wind, his howling was soon lost.

The next day, on his return, the flesher, chuckling and laughing, deposited a gory cloth upon the table, among the trenchers with which his niece was busied in preparing his noonday meal, and which, on being opened, displayed to her horrified gaze a freshly severed human hand enveloped in wolf-skin. Branda, comprehending what had occurred, shrieked aloud, shed a flood of tears, and then hurriedly throwing her mantle round her, whilst her uncle amused himself by turning and twitching the hand about with a ferocious delight, exclaiming, whilst he staunched the blood which still flowed:

'The sacristan said sooth; the wer-wolf has his need I trow, at last, and now I wot of his nature, I fear no more his witchcraft.'

Although the day was far advanced, Hugues lay writhing in torture upon his couch, his coverings drenched with blood, as well also the floor of his habitation; his countenance of a ghastly pallor, expressed as much moral, as physical pain; tears gushed from beneath his reddened eyelids, and he listened to every noise without, with an increased inquietude, painfully visible upon his distorted features. Footsteps were heard rapidly approaching, the door was hurriedly flung open, and a female threw herself beside his couch, and with mingled sobs and imprecations sought tenderly for his mutilated arm, which, rudely bound round with hempen wrappings, no longer dissembled the absence of its wrist, and from which a crimson stream still trickled. At this piteous spectacle she grew loud in her denunciations against the sanguinary flesher, and sympathetically mingled her lamentations with those of his victim.

These effusions of love and dolour, however, were doomed to sudden interruption; someone knocked at the door. Branda ran to the window that she might recognize who the visitor was that had dared to penetrate the lair of a wer-wolf, and on perceiving who it was, she raised her eyes and hands on high, in token of her extremity of despair, whilst the knocking momentarily grew louder.

"'Tis my uncle,' faltered she. 'Ah! woe's me, how shall I escape hence without his seeing me? Whither hide? Oh, here, here, nigh to thee, Hugues, and we will die together,' and she crouched herself into an obscure recess behind his couch. 'If Willieblud should raise his cleaver to slay thee, he shall first strike through his kinswoman's body.'

Branda hastily concealed herself amidst a pile of hemp, whispering Hugues to summon all his courage, who, however, scarce found strength sufficient to raise himself to a sitting posture, whilst his eyes vainly sought around for some weapon of defence.

'A good morrow to thee, Wulfric!' exclaimed Willieblud, as he entered, holding in his hand a napkin tied in a knot, which he proceeded to place upon the coffer beside the sufferer. 'I come to offer thee some work, to bind and stack me a faggot-pile, knowing that thou art no laggard at bill-hook and wattle. Wilt do it?'

'I am sick,' replied Hugues, repressing the wrath which, despite of pain, sparkled in his wild glance; 'I am not in fitting state to work.'

'Sick, gossip, sick, art thou indeed? Or is it but a sloth fit?

Hugues, the Wer-Wolf

Come, what ails thee? Where lieth the evil? Your hand, that I may feel thy pulse.'

Hugues reddened, and for an instant hesitated whether he should resist a solicitation, the bent of which he too readily comprehended; but in order to avoid exposing Branda to discovery, he thrust forth his left hand from beneath the coverlid, all imbrued in dried gore.

'Not that hand, Hugues, but the other, the right one. Alack, and well-a-day, hast thou lost thy hand, and I must find it for thee?'

Hugues, whose purpling flush of rage changed quickly to a death-like hue, replied not to this taunt, nor testified by the slightest gesture or movement that he was preparing to satisfy a request as cruel in its preconception as the object of it was slenderly cloaked. Willieblud laughed, and ground his teeth in savage glee, maliciously revelling in the tortures he had inflicted upon the sufferer. He seemed already disposed to use violence, rather than allow himself to be baffled in the attainment of the decisive proof he aimed at. Already had he commenced untying the napkin, giving vent all the while to his implacable taunts; one hand alone displaying itself upon the coverlid, and which Hugues, wellnigh senseless with anguish, thought not of withdrawing.

'Why tender me that hand?' continued his unrelenting persecutor, as he imagined himself on the eve of arriving at the conviction he so ardently desired – 'That I should lop it off? quick, quick, Master Wulfric, and do my bidding; I demanded to see your right hand.'

'Behold it then!' ejaculated a suppressed voice, which belonged to no supernatural being, however it might seem appertaining to such; and Willieblud to his utter confusion and dismay saw a second hand, sound and unmutilated, extend itself towards him as though in silent accusation. He started back; he stammered out a cry for mercy, bent his knees for an instant, and raising himself, palsied with terror, fled from the hut, which he firmly believed under the possession of the foul fiend.

Hugues, the Wer-Wolf

He carried not with him the severed hand, which henceforward became a perpetual vision ever present before his eyes, and which all the potent exorcisms of the sacristan, at whose hands he continually sought council and consolation, signally failed to dispel.

'Oh, that hand! To whom then, belongs that accursed hand?' groaned he, continually. 'Is it really the fiend's, or that of some wer-wolf? Certain 'tis, that Hugues is innocent, for have I not seen both his hands? But wherefore was one bloody? There's sorcery at bottom of it.'

The next morning, early, the first object that struck his sight on entering his stall, was the severed hand that he had left the preceding night upon the coffer in the forest hut; it was stripped of its wolf's-skin covering, and lay among the viands. He dared no longer touch that hand, which now, he verily believed to be enchanted; but in hopes of getting rid of it for ever, he had it flung down a well, and it was with no small increase of despair that he found it shortly afterwards again lying upon his block. He buried it in his garden, but still without being able to rid himself of it; it returned livid and loathsome to infect his shop, and augment the remorse which was unceasingly revived by the reproaches of his niece.

At last, flattering himself to escape all further persecution from that fatal hand, it struck him that he would have it carried to the cemetery at Canterbury, and try whether exorcism, and supulture in holy ground would effectually bar its return to the light of day. This was also done; but lo! on the following morning he perceived it nailed to his shutter. Disheartened by these dumb, yet awful reproaches, which wholly robbed him of his peace, and impatient to annihilate all trace of an action with which heaven itself seemed to upbraid him, he quitted Ashford one morning without bidding adieu to his niece, and some days after was found drowned in the river Stour. They drew out his swollen and discoloured body, which was discovered floating on the surface among the sedge, and it was only by piecemeal that they succeeded in tearing away from his death-contracted clutch, the phantom hand, which, in his suicidal convulsions he had retained firmly grasped.

A year after this event, Hugues, although minus a hand, and consequently a confirmed wer-wolf, married Branda, sole heiress to the stock and chattels of the late unhappy flesher of Ashford.

The Terror in the Snow

Hendry, my servant, saw to it that I should not forget Inspector Addington Peace. Shortly after the adventure which I have already narrated, I left London for a round of country visits. And if a paragraph concerning that eminent detective chanced to appear in a newspaper, the substance of it was brought to me with my shaving-water in the morning.

'I see as 'e 'as bin up to 'is games again, sir,' was Hendry's usual overture. 'My word, but 'e's a sly one, by all accounts,' was the customary conclusion.

I believe that Hendry often gained considerable notoriety in the servants' hall by a boasted friendship with Peace. To this I attribute the fact of his being consulted by Mr Heavitree's butler on the occasion of the burglary that took place while I was staying at Crandon. Hendry's ludicrous fiasco, which resulted in a lawsuit for false imprisonment, need not be narrated here, though it was considered a remarkably good joke against me at the time.

Towards the end of December, I returned to London for a few days, and on the third night after my arrival I decided to visit the inspector. Hendry had discovered that he was a bachelor, and lived in two little rooms on the third floor. The floors that separated us were let out as offices, so that Peace at the top and I at the bottom had the old house to ourselves after seven o'clock. The little man was at home, and seemed pleased to see me. With his sparrow-like agility he hopped about, producing glasses and a bottle of whisky. Finally, with our pipes in full blast, we sat facing each other across the fire, and soon dropped into a conversation which to me, at least, was of unusual interest. A very curious knowledge of London and its peoples, had Inspector Addington Peace.

An hour quickly slipped by, and when I rose to go I asked him if he would dine with me on my return from Cloudsham in Norfolk, where I was spending Christmas. He would be pleased, he told me;

and then, as he stooped to light a spill in the coals – 'You stay with the Baron Steen, I suppose?' he asked.

'Yes.'

'And why?'

'Why?' I echoed in some surprise.

'You have relatives or other friends?'

'My nearest relative is a sour old uncle in Bradford, who calls me hard names for using the gifts Providence gave me instead of adding up figures in a smoky office. As for friends – well, I am a fairly rich man, Inspector, and, as such, have many friends. What is there against the Baron Steen?'

'Oh, nothing,' he said, puffing at his pipe, so that he spoke as from a cloud, mistily.

'I know that he has played a bold game on the Stock Exchange,' I continued, 'and there may be a few outwitted financiers growling at his heels. But it would be hard to find a more thoughtful host. Yes, I am going to Cloudsham tomorrow.'

We shook hands warmly on parting, and as I descended the stairs he leant over the rail, smiling down upon me.

'Remember your dinner engagement,' I called up to him. 'I shall see you after the New Year.'

'Yes, if not before,' he said; and I seemed to catch the faint echo of a laugh as I turned the corner.

It was on the afternoon of December 24th that I stepped from the train at the little station of Cloudsham. Fresh snow had fallen, and the wind came bitterly over the frozen levels of the fen country. A distant clock was striking four as the carriage passed into the crested entrance-gates and tugged up a rising slope of parkland dotted with ragged oaks and storm-bowed spinneys, which showed as black stains upon its snow-clad undulations. At the summit the road bent sharply, and I saw below me the old manor of Cloudsham, beyond which – a sombre plain, losing itself in the evening mists that swathed the horizon – stretched the restless waters of the North Sea.

The house lay in a broad depression, in shape as the hollow of a hand, save only on the seaward side, where the line of cliff bit into it like the grip of a giant's teeth. The grey front looked up, across a slope of grass land, to a semicircle of forest that swept away in dark shadings of fir and oak. From the long oblong of the main buildings were thrust back two wings, flanked on the nearer side by a chapel.

THE TERROR IN THE SNOW

From the back of the house to the edge of the sea cliffs, a distance of some quarter of a mile, ran an irregular avenue of firs with clipped yew walks and laurel-edged flower gardens on either hand.

A dozen men sweeping the paths and a telegraph boy on a pony mounting the hill towards me showed as black pygmies against the drifts of snow.

My bachelor host was absent when I was ushered into the great central hall where the house-party were met together for their tea. I am by nature shy of strangers, taken in large doses, and it was with relief that I recognised Jack Talman, the grizzled cynic of an Academician, sitting in a corner seat well out of reach of draughts and female conversation.

'Hello, Phillips,' he welcomed me. 'And what financial gale brings you here?'

'What do you mean?'

'Don't put on frills with me. I've come to paint old Steen's picture, if he will give me the fifteen hundred that I'm asking for it. Lord Tommy Retford yonder is here to unload some of his old furniture – you know Tommy's rooms in Piccadilly, don't you? Furnished by a dealer in Bond Street, and twenty-five per cent. commission to Tommy on everything he can sell out of them. That's Mrs Talbot Slingsly talking to him. Pretty woman, got into trouble in New York, was cut by all America, and captured Slingsly and London Society at one blow. Scandal never does cross the Atlantic somehow – all the dirty linen gets washed in the herring-pond. That's old Lord Blane by the fire; very respectable, and lends money on the sly. "Private gentleman will make advances on note of hand" – you know. Fine woman Mrs Billy Blades – that's she on the sofa. She's been making desperate love to Steen, but no go. The gay old dog's too clever for her. That long chap's her husband. Watch him prowling round, looking to see if he can pouch a silver ashtray or something, I expect. By Jove, Phillips, but it's as good as a play, ain't it?'

'And this is London Society?' I exclaimed.

'No,' he cackled, shaking with vast amusement. 'No, man; no. It's the Smart Set, that advertised, criticised, glorious, needy brigade of rogues and vagabonds – the Smart Set. Bless 'em all, say I; they're the best of company, but it's as well to lock up your valuables before you become too intimate with them.'

I finished off my tea while old Talman sucked at his cigarette in great entertainment.

'You'd like to see the house,' he commenced again. 'Come along, I'll show you round – I want a walk before dinner.'

It was a most interesting ramble. We passed from room to room admiring the carved oak, the splendid pictures, the Sheraton furniture, the cabinets of old china, the armour, and the tapestry. For the manor was filled with the heirlooms of the de Launes, from whom the Baron Steen rented it. And though the present peer, a broken-down old drunkard, was living in a little villa at Eastbourne on eight hundred pounds a year, the family had been a great and glorious one, finding mention on many a page in English history.

At the end of the great dining-room, set in the black-oak wainscot above the fire, was the portrait of a boy. It was a Reynolds, and a worthy effort of that master hand. The lad could have been no more than fifteen years of age, but in his eyes was that grave, distracted expression that usually comes with the painful wisdom of later years. In more closely examining the picture, I noticed that a large portion of it at the bottom right-hand corner had been repaired or painted out. I called Talman's attention to this misfortune, asking if he knew the cause.

'They painted out the wolf,' he said, 'and with good enough reason, too.'

'A wolf?' I said.

'If old de Laune were to hear me gossiping about it he'd kick me out of the place – he would, by Jove! But with Steen in possession it's safe enough. Mind you, though, you mustn't mention it to the ladies – on your word, now.'

'Yes, yes,' I said eagerly; 'go on.'

'Such things frighten the women,' he explained. 'Well, it was in this way. Phillip, and he was the sixth earl, was our ambassador at St Petersburg somewhere about the year 1790. Once when he was out hunting he shot an old she-wolf that was peering from the mouth of a cave, and inside they found a thriving family of four cubs. One of them was white, an albino, I suspect. He saved it from the dogs and took it home. When he came back to Cloudsham the next year, he brought it along with his wife and his boy – an only son. They say it was a great pet at first, but it grew sulky with age, and finally was kept chained in the stables.

'One Christmas Eve, just as dusk was closing in, de Laune was trotting down the drive – he had been hunting at a distant meeting – when he heard a fearful screaming from the lower gardens towards the cliff. He put spurs to his horse, and in two minutes was galloping

THE TERROR IN THE SNOW

through the shadows of the fir avenue towards the sea. All of a sudden his horse pulled up dead, threw him, and bolted. When he got to his feet – he wasn't hurt, luckily – what did he see but the body of his son, lying with his throat torn out, and the white wolf standing over him, the broken chain dangling at its neck.

'They say he was a giant, this Philip de Laune, and of a very wild and passionate temper. Anyway, he went straight for the beast, and, though he was dreadfully mauled, he killed it – Heaven knows how – with his bare hands. That's why the present branch of the family came by the place. Pretty gruesome, isn't it?'

'A strange story,' I told him; 'but why must it be kept a secret from the ladies?'

'Because the beast walks, man. There's not a labourer in Norfolk who would go into the lower gardens on any night of the year, much less on Christmas Eve.'

'My good Talman, do you mean to say you believe this?'

'I don't know – but I wouldn't go into the lower gardens tonight, if I could walk round. Think of it, Phillips, the white shape with the bloody jaws lurking in the shadows! Ugh – let's go and get a cocktail before – '

'I beg your pardon, sir, but the Baron is looking for you.'

He was a tall, hatchet-faced fellow, with that mixture of respect and dignity that marks the well-trained British manservant. Upon the soft pile of the rugs we had not heard his footsteps.

'He asked me to find you, sir,' he continued, addressing himself to me with a slight bow. 'He is waiting in his room.'

As he preceded us thither, Talman whispered that Henderson – meaning thereby our conductor – was Steen's valet, and a very clever follow by all accounts.

The Baron, fat, high-coloured, and hearty, welcomed me with an open sincerity of pleasure well calculated to place a guest at his ease. A remarkable old boy was the Baron Steen. He always seemed to carry with him a jovial atmosphere of his own, in which those to whom he spoke were lost and blinded out of their better judgment. He was kind enough to pay me some compliments upon my watercolour work. Whatever else can be brought against him, no-one can deny that he was a sound judge of art. The dinner passed pleasantly enough that night, with free and witty conversation. Our bachelor host was in his most humorous mood, keeping those about him in shouts of laughter. Facing him, at the extremity of the long table, was his secretary, a thin, melancholy youth of about four-and-twenty.

My fair neighbour told me that Terry, as he was named, had been intended for the Church, but that his father, having ruined himself on the Stock Exchange, had persuaded the Baron to give him work. He was devoted to his patron, which, she smiled, was not surprising, seeing that he must be well on his way to rebuilding the fortune his father had lost.

I am not an ardent gambler, and when I do play I admit a preference for games in which brains are of some account. The roulette-table soon bored me, and after I had seen the last of a few pounds, I contented myself by watching the changing fortunes of the rest of the party. Just before eleven the Baron, who had parted with considerable sums of money in perfect good humour, excused himself, and before the rest had settled down to the table again, I slipped away to my bedroom, where a selection of novels and a favourite pipe offered more congenial attractions.

The room was of considerable size and majestically furnished. It was on the first floor at the extremity of the right-hand wing, and looked out over the gardens on the cliff. A branch road from the main drive ran beneath the windows to an entrance at the back of the house.

They had steam heat on the upper floors, and the high temperature of my room had drawn stale and heavy odours from the tapestry on the walls and the ancient hangings that fringed the huge four-post bedstead. It was the atmosphere of an old clothes shop on a July day. I pulled back the curtains, opened the window and thrust out my head for a mouthful of fresh air.

It was a quiet, moonless night, lit by the stars that blinked in their thousand constellations. Though the snow lay deep, the air struck mildly. Indeed, if it were freezing, it could not have been by more than two degrees. Upon the edge of the distant cliffs robes of confusing mist curled in veils as thin as moonlight; but in the foreground the yew walks and aisles of ancient laurel showed clearly upon the white carpet. About the central avenue of firs which carved the gardens into two the darkness lay in impenetrable pools of shadow. As I waited, the silence was startled by a bell. It rang the four quarters in a tinkling measure, followed by eleven musical strokes. I knew that the sound must come from the little church that lay to my right; but, though I leant from my window, the angle of the wing in which I was hid the building from me.

I feel that the story which I have now to tell may well turn me into an object for ridicule. I can only describe that which I saw; as for the conclusions at which I arrived there are many more practical people in the world than myself who would have judged no differently. At best it was a ghastly business.

I had returned to the dressing-table and was changing my dress-coat for a comfortable smoking-jacket when I heard it – a faint and distant cry, yet a cry which was crowded with such terror that I clung to a chair with my white face and goggling eyes staring back at me from the mirror on the table. Again it sounded, and again; then silence fell like the shutter of a camera. I rushed to the window, peering out into the night.

The great gardens lay sleeping in the dusky shadows. There was nothing to be heard; nothing moved save the curling wreaths of mist that came creeping up over the cliffs like the ghosts of drowned sailormen from their burial sands below. Could it have been some trick of the imagination? Could it – and the suggestion which I despised thrust itself upon me – could it bear reference to that grim tragedy that had been played in the old fir avenue so many years ago?

And then I first saw the THING that came towards me.

It was moving up a narrow path, hedged with yew, that led from the gardens and passed to the right of the wing in which I stood. The yew had been clipped into walls some five feet high, but the eastern gales had beaten out gaps and ragged indentations in the lines of greenery, so that in my sideways view of it the path itself was here and there exposed. It was through one of these breaches in the walls that I noticed a sign of movement. I waited, straining my eyes. Yes, there it showed again, a something, moving swiftly towards the house with a clumsy rolling stride.

It was never nearer to me than fifty yards, and the stars gave a shifty light. Yet it left me with an impression that it was about four feet in height and of a dull white colour. I remember that its body contrasted plainly with the dark hedges, but melted into uncertainty against a patch of snow. Once it stopped and half raised itself on its hind legs as if listening. Then again it tumbled forward in its shambling, ungainly fashion – now hidden by the yew wall, now thrust into momentary sight by a ragged gap until it disappeared round the angle of the house. Doubtless it would turn to the left, round the old chapel, across the snow-bound park, and so to the woods – where a wolf should be!

I was still staring from the window in the blank fear of the unknown, when I heard the swift tap of feet upon the road beneath me. Round the corner of the wing came a man, running with a patter of little strides, while a dozen yards behind him were a pair of less active followers. What they wanted I did not consider; for at that moment the sight of my own kind was joy enough for me. The electric lamps in the room behind me threw a broad golden patch upon the snow, and as the leader reached it he stopped, glancing up at where I stood. The light struck him fairly in the face. It was Addington Peace!

'Did you hear that cry?' he panted; and then, with a sudden nod of recognition: 'I see who it is. Mr Phillips – well, and did you hear it?'

'It came from over there – in the fir avenue,' said I, pointing with a trembling finger. 'I don't understand it, Inspector; I don't indeed. There was something that came up that yew walk behind you about a minute afterwards. I should have thought it would have passed you.'

'No, I saw nothing. What was it like?'

'A sort of a dog,' I stammered; for under his steady eye I had not nerve enough to tell him of my private imaginings.

'A dog – that's curious. Are all the rest of you in bed?'

'No; they're gambling!'

'Very good. I see there is a door at the back there. Will you come down and let me in, after I've had l look round the gardens?'

'Certainly.'

'If you meet any of your friends, you need not mention that I have arrived. Do you understand?'

I nodded, and he hopped away across the lawn with his two companions at his heels.

I slipped on an overcoat and made my way quietly down the stairs. From the roulette-room, as I passed it, came the chink of money and the murmur of merry voices. They would not disturb us, that was certain. I reached the garden doors in the centre of the main building, turned the key, and walked out into the gloom of a great square porch.

As I have said, the temperature was scarcely below freezing-point, and if I shivered in my fur-lined overcoat it was more from excitement than any great chill in the air. For a good twenty minutes I waited listening and peering into the night. It was not a pleasant time, for my nerves were jangled, and I searched the shadows with timorous eyes, half fearing, half expecting, Heaven knows what hideous apparition. It was with a start which set my heart thumping that I saw Peace turn the corner of the right-hand wing and come trotting down the drive towards me. There was something in his aspect that told a story of calamity.

'What is it?' I asked him, as he panted up.

'I want you – come along,' he whispered, and started back by the way he had come.

We passed round the right-hand wing, under my bedroom window, and stopped where the yew walk ended. To right and left of the entrance two stone fauns leered upon us under the starlight.

'This thing you call a dog – could you see it as far as this?'

'No; the angle of the wing prevented me.'

'You saw it pass in this direction. Are you certain it did not go back the way it came?'

'Yes. I am quite certain.'

'Then it must either have turned up the road, in which case I should have met it; or down the road, where you would have seen it as it passed under your windows; or else have run straight on. If we take these facts as proved, it must have run straight on.'

'That is so.'

We had our backs to the laughing fauns. Before us lay a broad triangle of even snow, with the chapel and wing of the house for its sides, and for its base the carriage-drive on which we stood. There was no shrub or tree in any part of it that might conceal a fugitive. Close to the wall of the house ran a path ending in a small side door. The chapel, which was joined to the mansion, had no entrance on the garden side.

'If it entered this triangle and disappeared – for I am certain it was not here when I ran by – we may conclude that it found its way into the house. It had no other method of escape. Kindly stay here, Mr Phillips. This snow is fortunate, but I wish the sweepers had not been so conscientious about their work on the paths.'

He drew a little electric lantern from his coat, touched the spring, and with an eye of light moving before him, turned into the path under the wall. He walked slowly, bending double as he swept the brilliant circle now on the exposed ground, now on the snow ridges to right and left. The sills of the ground-floor window were carefully examined, and when he reached the door he searched the single step before it with minute attention. A curious spectacle he made, this little atom of a man, as he peeped and peered his way like some slow-hunting beast on a cold scent.

It was not until he left the path for the snow-covered grass-plot that I saw him give any sign of success. He dropped on his knees with a little chirrup of satisfaction like the note of a bird. Then he rose again, shaking his head and staring up at the windows above him in a cautious, suspicions manner. Finally he came slowly back to me, with his head on one side, staring at the ground before him.

'You thought it was a dog?' he asked. 'Why a dog?'

'It looked to me like a big dog – or a wolf,' I told him boldly.

'Whether it be beast or man, or both, I believe the thing that killed him is in the house now.'

I jumped back, staring at him with a sudden exclamation. 'Who has been killed?' I stammered out.

'Baron Steen. We found him on the cliffs yonder. He was badly cut about.'

'It's impossible, Inspector,' I cried. 'He left the roulette-table not a quarter of an hour before you came.'

'Ah – he was a cool hand, Mr Phillips. It was like him to put off bolting till the last minute. The warrant against him for company frauds is in my pocket now. But someone gave the game away to him, for his yacht is lying off the beach there, with a boat from her waiting at the foot of the cliff. But we've no time to lose – come along.'

Before the big garden porch the inspector's two companions were waiting. He drew them aside for a minute's whispered conversation before they separated, and disappeared into the night. What had they done with the body? I had not the courage to inquire.

We entered the house, moving very softly. In the hall Peace took me by the arm.

'You're a bit shaken, Mr Phillips, and I'm not surprised. But I want your assistance badly. Can you pull yourself together and help me to see this through?'

'I'll do what I can.'

'Take me up to your room, then.'

We were in luck, for we tiptoed up the great stairs and down the long passages without meeting a guest or servant. Once in my room, the inspector walked across and pushed the electric bell. Three, four minutes went by before the summons was answered, and then it was by a flushed and disordered footman who bounced into the room and halted, staring openmouthed from me to my companion.

'Sorry to disturb your dance,' said Peace, beaming upon him.

'Beg pardon, sir, but you startled me – yes, we was 'aving a little dance in the servants' 'all; but it's of no consequence, sir.'

'A slippery floor, eh, with so much French chalk on it?'

The young man glanced at the powder on his shoes and grinned.

'So you are all dancing in the servants' hall, are you?'

THE TERROR IN THE SNOW

'I believe so, sir, barring Edward, who is waiting on the party, and Mr Henderson.'

'And where is Mr Henderson?'

'He is the baron's man, sir. I should not presume to inquire where he was. Beg pardon, sir, but are you staying here tonight?'

'This is a friend of mine,' I interposed. 'He will stay the night; but you need not trouble about that now.'

'A smart fellow like you can keep his mouth shut,' continued the inspector, sweetly. 'You wouldn't go shouting all over the house if you were let into a secret – now, would you?'

'Oh no, sir; on my word I wouldn't.'

And so Peace told him of the projected arrest, of the murder, and of his own identity. The colour faded from the young man's cheeks, but he stood stiff and silent, never taking his eyes from the little detective's face.

'And what can I do, sir?' he asked, when the tale was over. 'He was a good master to us, sir; whatever there was against him, he was good to us. You can trust me to help catch the scoundrel who killed him if I can.'

'I see this room is warmed by steam heat. Is that the case with all the bedrooms and passages?'

'Yes, sir. The only open fires are in the reception-rooms. When the baron made the alterations last year, they left the grates for the sake of appearance; but they are never lighted, save on the ground floor.'

'And in what reception-rooms are there fires at the present moment?'

'The dining-room fire has died out by now,' said the young man, ticking off the numbers on his fingers. 'But there is one in the big hall, one in the library where the party is playing, one in the little drawing-room, and one in the baron's room.'

'And the kitchen?'

'Of course, sir, one in the kitchen and one in the servants' hall.'

'That is all. Are you certain?'

'Quite certain, sir.'

'Good; and now for the bath-rooms.'

'The bath-rooms, sir?'

'Exactly.'

'There are two bath-rooms in each wing; some of the gentlemen have tubs in their own rooms besides.'

'Now, I think we know where we are,' said the inspector, briskly. 'No chance of the roulette party breaking up, is there?'

'Oh no, sir; not for another two hours, at least.'

'I want you to return, Mr Phillips, and try your luck at the tables for a spell,' he said, with a quick glance at me. 'It is now eleven thirty; be back in this room at twelve fifteen. I am going to take a walk round the house with our young friend here in the meanwhile. The baron had a secretary, I believe?'

'Yes, a man called Terry.'

'Bring him up with you when you come. I shall want a talk with him. Is all quite plain?'

'Yes,' I told him; and so we parted.

When I stepped into the roulette-room I stood for a moment blinking at the players like a yokel at a pantomime. The scene was to me something unreal, a clever piece of stage effect, with its flushed and covetous faces, its frocks and its diamonds, its piles of sparkling gold, and the cry of the banker as he twirled the wheel. How could they be doing this with that bloodstained patch on the cliff edge, with that unknown horror slinking through the snow – how could they be doing this if they were not acting a part! An odd figure I must have looked, if there had been anyone to notice me. But they were too eager in the game to hear the opening of the door, or to see who went and came. I walked over to the fireplace, lit a cigarette, and watched them, my nerves growing steadier in the merry chatter of tongues. They were all there, the men and women of that careless house-party, all there – save one who lay silent wherever they had laid him.

Half an hour had slipped by, until, at last, with an effort, I walked to the table and threw down two sovereigns on the red.

It won, and I laughed at the melancholy omen; not, perhaps, without an odd note in my voice, for the man over whose shoulder I leaned to gather my winnings glanced up with a startled expression. It was young Terry, the secretary; the very person I wanted to see.

'Anything the matter, Mr Phillips?' he asked. 'You're not looking very well.'

'Don't worry about me,' I told him. 'But I want a word with you in private.'

'Certainly – just one moment.'

He had been winning heavily, and it took him some time to crowd the banknotes into his pockets. A sovereign slipped from his fingers and rolled under the table as he rose; but he paid no attention to it.

'I have something to tell you. Can you come up to my room?' I asked him.

He hesitated, looking regretfully at the table, where Fortune had been so kind to him.

'It happens to be rather important,' I said.

He followed me without another word. I did not attempt to explain until we had passed up the stairs and through the corridors to my room. He seated himself on the great bed with a shiver of cold, drawing the heavy curtains about his shoulders. And there I told him the story from the beginning to the end, hiding nothing, not even my belief in the supernatural nature of the thing which I had seen.

He never moved, but his face grew so pale and drawn that towards the end it seemed as if it were a powdered mask that stared at me from the shadows of the curtains. 'My God,' he cried, and fell back upon the bed in a passion of hysterical tears.

I tried to help him, but he thrust me fiercely away, so I thought it best to let him get over it himself. He was still lying on the thick quilt, sobbing and shivering, when the door opened and Peace stepped into the room. I explained the situation in a hurried whisper; but when I turned again Terry had got to his feet and was watching us, clinging to the bed-post.

'This is Inspector Addington Peace,' I told him. 'Perhaps you can give him some information?'

'Not tonight,' he cried, 'don't ask me tonight, gentlemen. You cannot tell what this means to me; tomorrow, perhaps – '

He dropped down upon the bed, covering his face with his hands. He seemed a helpless sort of creature, and my heart went out to him in his calamity.

'A night's rest is what you want,' I said, patting him on the shoulder. 'Come, let me give you an arm.'

He took it at once, with a grateful glance, and I led him down the corridor, with Peace in sympathetic attendance. Fortunately, his room was in the same wing, so we had not far to go. When we reached it, he thanked us for our care of him. And so we left him, returning to my bedroom in silence, for, indeed, the scene had been a painful one.

'Peace,' I said, when the door had closed behind us, 'what was the thing I saw in the yew walk?'

He had seated himself in an easy-chair, and was polishing the bowl of a well-stained meerschaum pipe, with a silk pocket-handkerchief.

'I think you already have an explanation,' he answered cheerfully.

'If it amuses you to sneer at my superstition – '

'You refer to the legend of the de Launes. I have heard the story before, Mr Phillips; nor am I surprised that you believed it to be the ghost wolf.'

'I did – but now I want you to disprove it.'

'On the contrary, all my evidence supports your theory.'

I stared at him, with a creeping horror in my blood. I was beginning to be afraid – seriously afraid. Peace leant back in his chair, with his eyes, vacant in expression, fixed on the wall. He seemed rather to be arguing with himself than addressing a listener.

'Baron Steen,' he said, 'met with his death on an open path between a shallow duck-pond and a little pavilion. He had fought hard for life, had rolled and struggled with his enemy. There were four or five punctured wounds in his throat and neck, from which he had bled profusely. And now for the thing that killed him – whatever it was. It could not have fled down the cliff path, for the boat's crew waiting below had heard the screams, and had come running up by that way. They were with him when we arrived, and assured me they had seen nothing. It could not have turned to the right or left, for, though the paths had been swept clean – doubtless by the baron's orders, for he would not desire his way of escape to be easily traced – the snow on either side lay in unbroken levels. It could only have retired by the yew avenue, and it did not break through the hedge. That, again, the snow proved clearly. So we may take it that whatever the thing may have been which you saw – it killed Baron Steen; further, it escaped into the house – this, you will remember, we decided in the garden. Let us imagine it was a man – that you were deceived by the uncertain light. His clothes must of necessity have been drenched in blood. He could not have struggled so fiercely with his victim and escaped those fatal signs. Yet, he cannot have burned his clothes, for the fires are downstairs where people were passing. Nor can he have washed them, for neither the bathrooms nor the bedroom basins have been recently used. I have spent some time in searching boxes and wardrobes with no result. Stranger still, as far as my limited information goes, everyone in the house can prove an alibi – save two.'

'And who are they?' I asked eagerly.

'Mr Henderson, the baron's valet – and yourself.'

'Inspector Peace – ' I began angrily.

'Tut, tut, my dear Mr Phillips. I was merely stating the facts. Mr Henderson's case, however, presents an interesting feature, for he has run away.'

'Run away,' I said. 'Then that settles it.'

'Not altogether, I'm afraid. I think it is more a matter of theft than murder with Mr Henderson.'

I stared at him in silence as he sat there, with his little hands clasped upon his lap, a picture of irritating composure.

'Peace,' I said, struggling to control my voice. 'What are you hiding from me? It is something inhuman, unnatural that has done this dreadful thing.'

The little detective stretched himself, yawned, and then rose to his feet. 'I have no opinion except that I think you had better get to bed. Don't lock your door, for I may find time for an hour's sleep on your sofa before morning.'

The news was out after breakfast – the news that led to mild hysterics and scurrying lady's-maids to the packing of boxes, and the chastened sorrow of those gentlemen who owed the baron money. Through all the turmoil of the morning moved the little detective, the most sympathetic of men. It was he who apologised so humbly for the locked doors of the bathrooms; he who superintended the lighting of fires, and the making of the beds, and the packing of trunks for the station so closely that the housemaids were convinced that he entertained a secret passion for each one of them; it was he who announced Henderson's robbery of the gold plate, following it by information as to the culprit's arrest. The establishment had by this time become convinced that Henderson was the murderer, and breathed relief at the news.

They had brought the body of Baron Steen to the house early in the morning – it had been laid in the garden pavilion on its first discovery.

With death in so strange a form present amongst us, I was disgusted by the noise and bustle, the gossip and chatter amongst the guests of the dead man. I wandered off in search of the one person who had seemed sincerely affected by the news, the young secretary, Maurice Terry. He was nowhere to be found. A servant of whom I inquired told me that the secretary had kept to his bed, being greatly unnerved by the tragedy, and I strolled up the stairs again on an errand of consolation. The door was locked, and there came no answer to my continued tapping.

'Terry,' I called through the keyhole. 'It is I, Phillips; won't you let me in?'

'I have a key that will fit, if you will kindly stand aside,' suggested a modest voice.

I rose from my knees to find the inspector at my elbow.

'It would be a gross intrusion,' I told him. 'If he wishes to be alone with his sorrow, we have no right to disturb him.'

'He is seriously ill.'

'How did you discover that?'

'By borrowing a gardener's ladder and looking through his window. He is unconscious, or was ten minutes ago.'

A skilful twist or two with a bit of wire and the key was pushed from the lock. The duplicate opened the door. Peace walked into the room, and I followed at his heels.

On his bed, fully dressed, lay poor Terry, with a face paler than his pillows. His breath came and went in short, painful gasps. One hand strayed continuously about his throat, groping and plucking at his collar with feverish unrest. It was a very painful spectacle.

'I will send for a doctor at once,' I whispered, stepping to the bell. But Peace held up a warning hand.

'Come here,' he said, 'I have something to show you.'

With movements as tender as a woman's he unfastened the man's collar and slipped out the stud. Then he paused. The eyes that watched me had turned cold and hard.

'If it is as I suspect, you may be called as a witness. Do you object?'

'Yes; but I shall not leave you on that account?'

'Very well,' he said, as he opened the shirt and the vest beneath it. Smeared and patched in dark etching upon the white skin was a broad stain of blood, of dried and clotted blood, the life's blood of a man.

'He is wounded, Peace,' I cried. 'Poor fellow, he must have nearly bled to death.'

'Do not alarm yourself,' said the inspector, drily. 'It is the blood of Baron Steen.'

* * *

A week had gone by, and I was sitting alone in my Keble Street rooms, when Peace walked in, with a heavy travelling-coat over his arm. 'Thank Heaven, you have come at last,' I cried. 'How is Maurice Terry?'

'Dead – poor fellow,' he said, with an honest sorrow in his voice. 'Yet, after all, Mr Phillips, it was the best that could have happened to him.'

'And his story – the causes – the method?' I demanded.

'It has taken some hard work, but the bits of the puzzle are fitted together at last. You wish to hear it, I suppose?'

THE TERROR IN THE SNOW

'According to your promise,' I reminded him.

'It is a case of unusual interest,' he said. 'Though it bears a certain similarity to the Gottstein trial at Kiel in '89.'

He paused to light his big pipe, and then sat back in his chair, with his eyes fixed in abstract contemplation.

'I was convinced that the murderer was in the house; and that he had entered by the side door, towards which you had seen him pass. When studying the spot I made a discovery of some importance. Steen had left by the same exit. Also he had reason to fear some person in that wing, for he had turned from the path and made a circuit over the grass. I had already noted his broad-toed boots when examining his body – and the footprints in the snow were unmistakable. Who was his enemy in that wing? It was a problem to be solved.

'I discovered no stained clothing, and no signs of its cleansing or destruction. From what information I could gather, all the house party had been in the roulette-room save yourself; and all the servants had been at the dance save Henderson and a man waiting on the guests. But in the course of my search the footman who accompanied me discovered that a quantity of gold plate was missing. It was reasonable to imagine that Henderson was the thief. Probably the confidential valet had learnt of the Baron's projected flight and of the warrant for his arrest. It was a moment for judicious robbery, the traces of which would be covered by the confusion of the news. But was Henderson also a murderer? I did not think so. The death of his master was the one thing which would wreck his scheme. In the early morning I interviewed the farmer on whose cart he had driven into Norbridge. He told me that, acting on orders he had received from Henderson, he met that person at the corner of the stables at eleven o'clock precisely – five minutes before the murder occurred. That finally eliminated the valet from the list.

'On my return from the farm I examined the gardens again with great minuteness. At the corner of the little pavilion, about fifteen feet from where the body had lain, there was a patch of bloody snow. This puzzled me a good deal, until the solution offered itself that the murderer had tried to wash his hands in the snow, the water of the pond being frozen hard. Yet his clothing would also bear the stain. What had he worn that showed so white to you in the starlight? Could it have been that he wore no clothes at all?'

A naked man! The suggestion was full of possibilities.

'It was fortunate that I had brought assistants to help me in Steen's capture. Their presence gave me a wider scope, for they were both good men. I left them to search the pavilion and laurels for the clothing, which the murderer might have concealed when he realised how fatal was its evidence. As I walked back to the house I began to understand the situation more clearly. The main drive, curving down the slope of the park, was in view of a tall man coming up by the yew walk. The murderer might have noticed our approach. What more natural than that he should have bent double as he ran, thus obtaining the cover of the left-hand hedge, which was not more than four to five feet high? Did not this answer to your description of the thing you had seen? It would have been cold work for him. I made a note to be on the lookout for chills.

'For a couple of hours I devoted myself to speeding those guests who caught the eleven-thirty train. I do not think a trunk left for the station of which I have not a complete inventory. Indeed, the baron's creditors have to thank me for the return of several trifles of value, which were included, accidentally, no doubt, in the ladies' dressing-bags.

'After the carriages had started I went in search of Terry, and discovered that he had not left his room. Equally to the point, his windows looked down upon the spot where the baron made his detour over the grass while escaping.

I became interested in this young man. The score was creeping up against him. A ladder from an obliging gardener allowed me to observe him from the window. A visit to the housekeeper gave me a duplicate hey to his door. What happened in the room you know, Mr Phillips.'

'But, the motive – why did he kill his patron?' I asked him eagerly.

'I doubt if we shall ever learn the truth on that point,' he said. 'As far as I can make out, Steen was directly responsible for the ruin and disgrace of Terry's father. Probably the son did not fully realise this when the baron, with a pity most unusual in the man, gave him the secretaryship. But of all participation in the flight he was certainly innocent, for he was in bed at the time.'

'In bed!' I cried.

'Don't interrupt, if you please. What happened I take to be as follows: Terry was in bed when the old man tried to creep past his window. Somehow he heard him, and, looking out, understood what was up. Perhaps that rascal Henderson had told him the truth about his father; perhaps Steen had promised him compensation – he had a mother and sister dependent on him – which promise the financier meant to avoid, along with many more serious obligations, by running away. At any rate, passion, revenge, the sense of injustice – call it what you like – took hold of the lad. He caught up the first handy weapon, it chanced to be a dagger paper-knife – dangerous things, I hate them – and rushed down a back staircase and through the side door in pursuit of his enemy.

'When that had happened which happened, the fear that comes to all amateurs in crime took him by the throat. He wiped his hands in the snow; he tore off his sleeping suit – that is how I know he had been in bed – and thrust it, with its terrible evidences of murder, into the thatch of the little pavilion. We found it there a day later. Then he started back to the house as naked as a baby.

'He saw us running down the hill, and made for the side door, bending double behind the hedge. Who were we? Had we noticed him? Believe me, Mr Phillips, whether he had held the murder righteous or no, it was only the rope he saw dangling before him. Might not the alarm be given at any moment? He dared not wash himself, and the stains had dried upon him. He hurried on his clothes, shivering in the chill that had struck home, and so to the safest place he could find – the roulette-table.'

'It is well that he died,' I said simply.

'It saved the law some trouble,' remarked the inspector, with a grim little nod at the wall.

England and Wales, Scotland and Ireland

IT is undoubtedly far more difficult for those living to-day to imagine the old England of peace and prosperity, than it is for those of us who remember our country before the dawning of the twentieth century to trace in our minds a similar picture. And even fifty years since, when we travelled at leisure and in security through some of the wilder parts of the kingdom, we could scarce believe that such a journey as we were taking under so pleasant and easy conditions was once an enterprise fraught with considerable danger owing to the numbers of ferocious animals that infested the very woods and glens and moors we were thus serenely traversing.

To-day the risks are no less than in ancient times, the British and Anglo-Saxon periods, although truly the perils are of a different kind. From one end of our island to another the roads are packed and ploughed by mechanical conveyances of the ugliest and most vicious pattern, swift engines of death and destruction, goaded to a maniac speed amid stench unutterable and the din of devils.

When we see London, despoiled of all her beauty, her nakedness uncovered, throwing out hideous suburban tentacles for mile after mile on all sides, it is impossible to realize that between the tenth and twelfth centuries there came up wellnigh to her gates, but a few fair meadows and open pasture lands intervening, vast forests in whose depths dwelt the stag, and the wild-boar and the bull.

Even at a comparatively modern period nearly the whole of the county of Stafford was either moor or woodland. Cannock Chase alone measured no less an expanse than 36,000 acres. " The moorlands is the more northerly mountainous part of the county, lying betwixt Dove and Trent. . . . The woodlands are the more southerly, level part of the county, being from Draycote to Wichnor, Burton, etc. Between the aforesaid rivers, including Needwood-forest,

ENGLAND, WALES, SCOTLAND, IRELAND

with all its parks, are also the parks of Wichnor, Chartley, Horecross, Bagots, Loxley, Birchwood, and Paynesley (which anciently were all but as one wood, that gave it the name of woodlands)."[1] Maxwell forest, near Buxton, with the great forest of Macclesfield, the Peak forest, and the high Derbyshire moors united to make up " that mountainous and large featured district which in ancient times had been well timbered and formed part of the great midland forest of England ".[2] From Nottingham to Manchester, and thence far on into Yorkshire, was one continuous forest, and there came to meet it the even wilder and larger forest of Bowland.

In Scotland all the district between Chillingham and Hamilton, some eighty miles, was completely wooded, and further north lay the huge Caledonian forest itself.

Inadequate and readily to be supplemented as are these few haphazard details, they will perhaps suffice to show what magnificent tracts of unreclaimed forest-land once existed here, affording through centuries an impenetrable fastness for wild beasts, and especially for the wolves whom year after year it seemed wellnigh impossible to exterminate and dislodge.

The forests of Reedsdale in Northumberland; Blackburnshire and Bowland in Lancashire; Richmond Forest comitatu Ebur; Sherwood Forest, Nottinghamshire; Savernake Forest in Wilts; the New Forest; the forests of Bere and Irwell; and many more are recorded as being the strongholds of packs of the most swift and savage wolves.

Of all British animals that have become extinct within historic memory the wolf was the last to disappear.[3]

Wolf-hunting was a favourite pursuit of the ancient Britons, and legend tells how wicked Mempricius (or Memprys), one of the descendants of old King Brute, a monarch who may have ruled Albion about 980 B.C., in that year fell a prey to the wolves whom he delighted to hunt with his great hounds, as old Andrew of Wyntoun [4] sings:—

> His brother he slew and syne all thai
> That he trowit wald thaim ma
> For to succeid till him as king.
> It happinnit syne at a hunting
> With wolffis him weryit to be;
> Sa endit his iniquite.

Verstegan (Richard Rowlands), in his *Restitution of Decayed Intelligence in antiquities*,[5] writes of the Saxons: "The moneth which wee now call *Ianuary* they called *Wolf-monat*, to wit *Wolf-moneth*, because people are wont alwayes in that moneth to bee in more danger to bee deuowred of wolues, then in any season els of the yeare; for that through the extremitie of cold & snow, those rauenous creatures could not fynd of other beasts sufficient to feed vpon."

It is not without significance that in the *Poenitentiale*[6] of Egbert, Archbishop of York, who died 766, it is prescribed that "if a wolf shall attack cattle of any kind, and the animal so attacked shall thereof die, no Christian may eat of it". It would appear as though the wolf imparted by his very bite some demoniac quality to the beeves he had torn and slain.

Speaking of Flixton near Filey in Yorkshire, Camden[7] records that here " in King Athelstanes time was built an *Hospitall, for the defense* (thus word for word it is recorded) *of way-faring people passing that way from Wolues, least they should bee devoured*. Whereby it appeereth for certaine, that in those daies Wolues made foule worke in this tract, which now are no where to be seene in England, no not in the very marches toward Scotland; and yet within Scotland there be numbers of them in most places".

When Athelstan in 938 won so signal a victory at Brunanbrugh over Constantine, King of Wales, he imposed upon the defeated a yearly tribute of money, cattle, hawks, and keen-scented dogs, which mulct of gold and silver his successor, King Edgar, permitted Ludwall (or Idwal), the heir of Constantine, to exchange for the pelts of 300 wolves. It is generally stated that Edgar did this " to the intent the whole Countrie might once be clensed and clerely ridde " of these ravenous creatures, " whose carcases being brought into Lloegres, were buried at Wolfpit, in Cambridgeshire, and by that meanes thereof within the compasse and terme of foure yeres, none of those noysome creatures were left within Wales and England. Since this tyme also we read not that anye Wolfe hath beene seene here that hath bene bredde within the bondes and limites of our country."[8] The legend certainly grew and stuck fast that in this way

ENGLAND, WALES, SCOTLAND, IRELAND

the wolves were utterly exterminated, as poets loved to repeat. Thus Michael Drayton, in his *Polyolbion*,[9] 1612, the ninth song, has :—

> Thrice famous *Saxon* King, on whom Time nere shall pray,
> O *Edgar!* who compeldst our *Ludwall* hence to pay
> Three hundred Wolues a yeere for trybute vnto thee :
> And for that tribute payd, as famous may'st thou bee,
> O conquer'd *British* King, by whom was first destroy'd
> The multitude of Wolues, that long this Land annoy'd.

In his note Selden is careful to remark : " But this was not an vtter destruction of them ; for, since that time, the Mannor of *Piddlesey* in *Leicester* shire was held by one *Henry* of *Augage*, per serjeantiam capiendi lupos, as the inquisition deliuers it." [10]

Edward Ravenscroft prefixed as a Preface to his tragicomedy *King Edgar and Alfreda*,[11] acted at the Theatre Royal late in 1677, " *The* Life *of* Edgar, *King of the* West Saxons," in which the tribute he imposed upon the Princes of Wales " To clear the Land from Wolves " is duly recorded, but there is no reference to this in the play as we should perhaps have expected, and it is rather surprising that there is no mention of wolves in Thomas Rymer's unacted " Heroick Tragedy ", *Edgar, or The English Monarch*.[12]

William Somervile, in *The Chace* (1735),[13] has the following reference to " glorious Edgar " :—

> Wise, potent, gracious Prince !
> His Subjects from their cruel Foes he sav'd,
> And from rapacious Savages their Flocks.
> *Cambria's* proud Kings (tho' with Reluctance) paid
> Their tributary Wolves ; Head after Head,
> In full Account, 'till the Woods yield no more,
> And all the rav'nous Race extinct is lost.

Even so serious and careful an author such as Dr. John Caius, in his *De Canibus Britannicis*, 1570,[14] when treating of the Sheep-Dog *Canis Pastoralis*, and taking occasion to mention the tribute paid to Edgar, quite confidently wrote that our shepherd's dog " hath not to deal with the bloud thyrsty wolf, sythence there be none in England, which happy and fortunate benefite is to be ascribed to the puisaunt Prince *Edgar* . . . Synce which time we reede that no Wolfe hath bene seene in England, bred within the bounds and borders of this countrey ". He seems to have been little

aware that the wolf had not become entirely extinct in
England three-quarters of a century before, and did not
entirely vanish from the British Isles until 200 years after
his own day.

It is hardly necessary to review the ample evidence which
shows the abundance of wolves in England during the period
from the Norman Conquest until the beginning of the
sixteenth century.

Guido, Bishop of Amiens, in his *Carmen de Bello
Hastingensi*,[15] quite naturally relates that the Conqueror
left the dead bodies of the English on the battle-field to rot
and be devoured by beasts of prey :—

> uermibus, atque lupis, auibus canibusque uoranda,
> deserit Anglorum corpora strata solo.

The New Forest and the Forest of Bere, which, as we have
noted, both teemed with wolves, were favourite hunting-
grounds of the Red King and Henry I. It is chronicled in
the *Annales Cambriae* [16] that in 1166 a mad wolf bit two and
twenty persons, all of whom in a short space died.

In the reign of King John is said to have occurred the
well-known circumstance of faithful Gellert being rashly
slain by Prince Llewellyn, a story so familiar as it were
superfluous to relate.[17]

Henry III not infrequently made grants of lands to various
individuals upon the condition that these owners should
hunt down and destroy the menacing wolves. Similar
notices are found during the reigns of the three Edwards,
Richard II, and the three Henries.

In his *Boke of Saint Albans*,[18] written about 1480 and
printed at Saint Albans by the Schoolmaster-Printer in
1486, Dame Juliana Berners (or Barnes) includes the wolf
among the " Bestys of venery " :—

> Wheresoeuere ye fare by fryth or by fell
> My dere chylde take hede how Tristram dooth you tell
> How many maner beestys of venery ther were
> Lystyn to yowre dame and she shall yow lere
> Fowre maner beestys of venery there are
> The first of theym is the . hert . the secunde is the hare
> The boore is oon of tho . the Wolff and not oon moo.

There is hardly any hint afforded here that the wolf is
becoming a particularly scarce animal, although relentless

ENGLAND, WALES, SCOTLAND, IRELAND

war had been waged against him from all sides for long enough. An old, but apparently unsupported, tradition says that the last wolf in England was killed at Wormhill Hall near Buxton in the county of Derby, and certainly it is probable that the royal Forest of the Peak, wild and of vast extent, would afford cover for the remnant of this savage tribe. Be that as it may, the reign of King Henry VII is certainly to be assigned as the term of the period to which the wolf lingered here. Seventy years or so later George Turbervile in his *Booke of huntynge* writes : " The Wolfe is a beaste sufficiently knowen in Fraunce and other Countries where he is bred : but here in Englād they be not to be foūd in any place. In Ireland (as I haue heard) there are great store of them." [19]

Long after he had been extirpated in England the wolf continued to be " rycht noysum to the tame bestiall in all partis of Scotland ".[20] Camden at the end of the sixteenth century remarks that Strath-Navern, "the utmost and farthest coast of all Britaine," is " sore haunted and annoied by most cruell wolues ", who not only set upon cattle but also " assaile men with great danger, and not in this tract onely, but in many other parts likewise of Scotland ".[21] But a hundred years after Sir Robert Sibbald avers that the animal had been wholly exterminated. Although their numbers were no doubt greatly diminished, especially after the great hunts arranged in the days of James V (born 1512, died 1542) and Queen Mary, his daughter, actually it was not until the year 1743 that the last of the species was destroyed at a remote spot between Fi-Giuthas and Pall-à-chrocain.

One winter day the Laird of MacIntosh was apprised that a large " black beast " supposed to be a wolf had been descried prowling in the glens, and less than twenty-four hours before had killed two children who were crossing the hills from Calder. A " Tainchel " or general drive was at once proclaimed, and amongst others summoned to the meet not the least important was a famous deer-stalker, MacQueen, who had the fleetest and strongest hounds in the country. All assembled at the tryst had waited long impatiently expecting MacQueen's arrival ere he appeared on the scene. MacIntosh began to upbraid his unusual tardiness, when for answer the hunter lifted his plaid and threw the bleeding head of the wolf at the laird's feet, to be overwhelmed with congratulations and well feed in a generous gift of land for his prowess.[22]

Even later did the wolf maintain his hold upon Ireland, where formerly he existed in such numbers that a special breed of dog, a tall rough greyhound of exceptional size and power, and most highly esteemed, the Irish Wolf-hound, was especially reared to hunt the fierce and fearful packs. "They are not without woolues and grayhoundes to hunt them, bigger of bone and limme then a colt," says Holinshed in his description of Ireland,[23] and Camden writes, "much noisance they have everywhere by Wolues." Thus in the *Travels of Cosmo the Third, Grand Duke of Tuscany, through England*[24] in 1669, wolves are spoken of as common in Ireland, which indeed had acquired and long kept the nickname of "Wolf-land".

"Wolves still abound too much in Ireland," Harting quotes from *The Present State of Great Britain and Ireland*, 1738; and in an article on the Irish Wolf-dog printed in *The Irish Penny Journal* for 1841,[25] Mr. H. D. Richardson says: "I am at present acquainted with an old gentleman between eighty and ninety years of age, whose mother remembered Wolves to have been killed in the county of Wexford about the years 1730–1740, and it is asserted by many persons of weight and veracity that a Wolf was killed in the Wicklow Mountains so recently as 1770."

In his *Origins of English History*[26] Charles Isaac Elton draws attention to the fact that there was no more usual periapt among the ancient Britons than "crescents made of the wolf's teeth and boars' tusks perforated and worn as charms". He also remarks, "We know that at one time the wolves swarmed in Sherwood and Arden"; and emphasizes that "the wolf and wild boar lingered until the end of the seventeenth century in the more remote recesses of the island", a generalization which is perhaps not strictly accurate, since, as we have seen, the wolf in England was extinct early in the sixteenth century, and in Scotland was not finally destroyed until the fourth decade of the eighteenth.

That werewolfism was a sorcery not unpractised by Anglo-Saxon warlocks is very certain, although the records are

ENGLAND, WALES, SCOTLAND, IRELAND

neither numerous nor detailed. It is not surprising that many erroneous beliefs had grown up concerning these demoniac wolves which the Bishops and priests were at some pains to correct.

In an old *Poenitentiale Ecclesiarum Germaniae*,[27] 151, occurs the following: " Hast thou believed what some were once wont to hold, namely that those who are commonly called *Parcae* can effect what they are often supposed to effect, namely that when a man is born they can direct and achieve his destiny, and moreover by a magic spell whensoever certain men will they are able to transform themselves into wolves, and such a one of this kind is called (*teutonica*) ' Werewulff ',[28] or else they transform themselves into another animal shape as they list. If thou hast believed that Man made in God's Image and Likeness can be essentially changed into another species or form by any power save that of Almighty God alone, thou must fast therefor ten days on bread and water."

In England a precisely similar clause, xv — " whosoever shall believe that a man or woman may be changed into the shape of a wolf or other beast . . ."— occurs in the *Poenitentiale* [29] (1161-2) of Bartholomew Iscanus, Bishop of Exeter, who died 1184. It should be carefully remarked that no denial of werewolfism is implied, that was far too real and too terrible a sorcery, but it is insisted that there must be a right theological understanding of this dark matter. For many had been reduced into giving the Devil an almost unlimited power, and thus betrayed into the most horrid impiety.

Although it has already been quoted, we may not impertinently remind ourselves of the well-known passage in Gervase of Tilbury's *Otia Imperialia*, written during the years 1210-14, where he speaks of the English werewolves, men who are thus metamorphosed at the changes of the moon,[30] adding that such shape-shifting was then by no means uncommon in this island. He returns to the same subject a little later in his work, and chapter cxx [31] is sufficiently important to be quoted in full: " *Of men, who were wolves.* It is often debated among the learned whether Nabuchodonosor during the allotted time of his penance was indeed essentially metamorphosed into an ox, since all theologians agree that 'twere easier to transform one shape into another than to create out of nothing. Some authors have written that he acted as an ox, and as a beast ate grass and hay, being an ox in all things his shape excepted. One thing I know that among us it is certain there are men who at certain waxings of the moon are transformed into wolves. In Auvergne—(the facts came under my personal observation)—a part of the diocese of Clermont, a certain great noble, Ponce de Castres, outlawed and exiled Raimbaud de Poinet, a valiant soldier, who had long carried arms. When thus banished and become a wanderer on the face of the earth, what time Raimbaud was wandering all alone, as if he had been some wild animal, making his weary way through trackless and untrodden paths, it happened that one night there fell upon him a damp and sore amaze, and he grew frantic being changed into a wolf, under which shape he marauded his own native village, so that the farmers and franklins in terror abandoned their cottages and manors, leaving them empty and tenantless. This fearsome wolf devoured children, and even older persons were attacked by the beast, which tore their flesh grievously with its keen and savage teeth. At last a certain carpenter was bold enough to attack the aggressor, and with a swift blow of his axe lopped off one of the beast's hind paws, whereupon the werewolf at once resumed human shape. Raimbaud publicly acknowledged that he was right glad thus to lose his foot, since such dismembering had rid him for ever of the accursed and damned form. For it is commonly reported and held by grave and worthy doctors that if a werewolf be shorn of one of his members he shall then surely recover his original body.

" In the neighbourhood of Chalus, in the diocese of Mende and the department of Ardèche, there lived a man, Calcevayra by name, who was a werewolf. Now he at the plenilune was wont to go apart to a distant spot and there stripping himself mother-naked he would lay all his clothes under some sheltered rock or thornbush. Next, nude as he was, he rolled to and fro in the sand until he rose up in the form of a wolf, raging with a wolf's fierce appetites. With gaping jaws and lolling tongue he rushed violently upon his prey, and he used to explain that wolves always run with open

ENGLAND, WALES, SCOTLAND, IRELAND

mouths because this helps them to sustain their fleetness of foot. If they close their mouths they cannot easily unclench their teeth, wherefore they are more likely to be captured if by any chance they are pursued."

It were to be wished that, deeply interesting as are the histories he relates, Gervase of Tilbury had given us examples of werewolfism—and he must have known plenty of such instances—from England rather than from the south of France. It should be remarked that there exists from very ancient times a certain connection between the wolf and outlawry, the ritual of this procedure being essentially religious in character, as was clear enough from the ceremonial employed. In the *Lex Salica* of the old Franks we have the phrase: " wargus sit," " propie est, *eiectus, exue* " as Dom Bouquet glosses.[32] An early Norman Law prescribes as the punishment of certain crimes " wargus esto ", which is to say " Become a wolf ", so that anyone may pursue and slay the criminal, cutting him down as if he were a wolf, a savage beast.[33] The Laws of S. Edward the Confessor (about 1050), " De Hiis qui Pacem Ecclesie fregerint," concerning fugitives from justice have: " Et si postea repertus fuerit et teneri possit, uiuus regi reddatur, uel caput ipsius si se defenderit; lupinum enim caput geret a die ut lagacionis sue, quod ab Anglis wluesheued nominatur. Et hec sententia communis est de omnibus ut lagis." [34] A statute of Henry I runs: " Et si quis corpus in terra, uel noffo, uel petra, sub pyramide uel structura qualibet positum, sceleratus infamacionibus effodere uel exspoliare presumpserit, wargus habeatur." [35] In *The Tale of Gamelyn*,[36] a spurious poem which Urry added to the list of Chaucer's works and Tyrwhitt removed, these lines occur in reference to Gamelyn being outlawed :—

Tho were his bonde-men . Sory and nothing glad,
When Gamelyn her lord . wolves-heed was cryed and maad.

A later instance of this word occurs in one of the Towneley plays, *The Buffeting* [37] (c. 1460), where raging Caiaphas cries :—

Now wols-hede and out-horne on the be tane !

During the autumn of 1216 King John Lackland was ravaging the eastern counties of England. On 3rd October he sacrilegiously pillaged the church of good S. Guthlac at Croyland, after which, having lost all his baggage and many of his men in crossing the Welland, he pushed on in a black rage to the Cistercian abbey of Swineshead, near Bolton, where he surfeited himself by supping to excess on peaches and a kind of March ale. An attack of dysentery followed with fever. None the less he had himself conveyed to Newark, where he arrived on the sixteenth, by which time it became evident that the end was rapidly approaching. His physician, the Abbot of Croxton, shrived and houselled the dying king, who expired on the nineteenth of the month. As his will directed, he was buried in Worcester Cathedral, before the high altar.

At once strange legends began to fly abroad. In *The Brut, or The Chronicles of England*,[38] chapter clv, we already have the fully developed story of a monk at Swineshead, who appalled at the king's wickedness and the famine he swore to bring on England, went forth into the garden, where he found a toad which he pierced with a pin through and through till the venom had wholly infected a cup of lordly make. This he took and filled with humming ale, which he brought to John before whom he bent the knee lowlily, saying, " Sir, Wassail ! for never days of your life drank you of such a cup." " Begin, monk," quoth the king. So the monk drank a draught, and the king drained the goblet after him. Then the monk incontinently repaired to the infirmary, and presently breathed his last. On whose soul God have mercy. Amen ! And dirige with requiem shall be sung for him so long as the Abbey stands. But the bad king died within a few days, on the morrow after S. Luke.

Other chroniclers tell a different tale. Walter of Hemingburgh, the Austin Canon of Our Lady of Gisburn, writes how the lewd king, hearing that the Abbot of Swineshead had an exceedingly fair and virtuous sister, dispatched his pandars to bring her to him, being determined to enjoy her. Whereupon a monk of the house poisoned certain goodly pears of which the monarch ate, but not without first requiring the donor to eat of them also.[39]

The story that King John was poisoned by a monk of Swineshead has passed into the great body of Protestant tradition and even to-day is sometimes repeated. That

ENGLAND, WALES, SCOTLAND, IRELAND

half-crazed furious fanatic John Bale did not neglect to use it in his clouterly play *King Johan*,[40] the original draft of which was probably penned about 1538-1540 and considerably revised some two and twenty years later. Bale has the effrontery to hold up King John as a great and good monarch, a very father of his country. The legend of the poison furnishes a dramatic episode in *The Troublesome Raigne of King John*,[41] a foul and odious polemic, but the genius of Shakespeare utterly rejected the thing, even at the expense of losing what might well have been some powerful and not ineffective scenes.[42]

The story, however, which concerns us is that the evil monarch could not sleep in his tomb betwixt the shrines of S. Oswald and S. Wulstan,[43] those two blessed prelates, to the latter of whom in dying he had particularly recommended his soul.[44] Walter of Hemingburgh tells us, however, that he might not rest in his buriels.[45] Terrible noises, shrieks, howling, and other nocturnal disturbances were heard about the haunted grave,[46] until at last the Canons of Worcester disinterred his accursed body and flung the vile carcass, which had been embalmed by the Abbot of Croxton, out of the sanctuary on to a tract of unconsecrated ground, and he was verily Lackland whose rotting corse, the blackened features distorted in a hideous grin, had not even six foot of earth for a grave. But after death he became a werewolf,[47] and was seen abroad in this horrid shape, so that all men were greatly afraid. It is very curious that King John should become a werewolf after death, and one suspects there may be some confusion here, and that he became a vampire. For, as we know, in Germany, Serbia, and modern Greece it is believed that a werewolf is doomed to be a vampire after death.

Actually very few accounts of werewolfism in England and Scotland have survived. Mr. Elliott O'Donnell[48] gives an instance of a werewolf haunting in Cumberland, where in a newly-built house far from any town a phantom " nude and grey, something like a man with the head of a wolf—a wolf with white pointed teeth and horrid, light eyes ", was seen. There had previously been disturbances and howlings heard in the vicinity of the house. In a cave among the hills hard by were discovered a number of bones, among which was a wolf's skull and a human skeleton lacking the head. These were burned, and the hauntings ceased.

The same author mentions " the tall grey figure of a man with a wolf's head ", a ghost seen in the Valley of the Doones, Exmoor. He records a similar phantom as having appeared in a lonely district of Merionethshire, and speaks of two particular spots in Wales, " one near Iremadac and the other on the Epynt Hills, where, local tradition still has it, werewolves once flourished."

There has been related to me the story of a werewolf incident [49] which occurred in the late eighties of the last century. An Oxford professor, being an ardent fisherman, had taken a small cottage for the summer on the shores of one of the remoter lakes in Merionethshire, among the hills, and here he and his wife were entertaining a guest. Whilst wading one day a few yards into the lake he stumbled over an object which seemed upon examination to be the skull of a dog belonging to an uncommonly large breed. Desirous of investigating further he carried it back to the house, where it was temporarily placed on a kitchen shelf. That evening his wife had been left alone awhile, and to her surprise not unmixed with fear she heard a snuffling and scratching at the kitchen door which led into the yard. Hesitant lest she should be confronted with a fierce dog, she went into the room to make sure the door was barred. As she moved something drew her attention to the window, and there she saw glaring at her through the diamond panes the head of a huge creature, half animal, half human. The cruel panting jaws were gaping wide and showed keen white teeth ; the great furry paws clasped the sill like hands ; the red eyes gleamed hideously ; it was the gaze of a man, horribly intensive, horribly intelligent. Half-fainting with fear she ran through to the front door and shot the bolt. A moment after she heard heavy breathing outside and the latch rattled menacingly. The minutes that followed were full of acutest suspense, and now and again a low snarl would be heard at the door or window, and a sound as though the creature were endeavouring to force its entrance. At last the voices of her husband and his friend, come back from their ramble, sounded in the little garden ; and as they knocked, finding the door fast, she was but able to open ere she fell

ENGLAND, WALES, SCOTLAND, IRELAND

in a swoon at their feet. When her senses returned, to find herself laid on the sofa and her husband anxiously bending over her, she told in halting accents what had happened. That night, having made all secure and extinguished the lamps, the two men sat up quietly, armed with stout sticks and a gun. The hours passed slowly, until when all was darkest and most lonely the soft thud of cushioned paws was heard on the gravel outside, and nails scratched at the kitchen window. To their horror in a stale phosphorescent light they saw the hideous mask of a wolf with the eyes of a man glaring through the glass, eyes that were red with hellish rage. Snatching the gun they rushed to the door, but it had seen their movement and was away in a moment. As they issued from the house a shadowy undefined shape slipped through the open gate, and in the stars they could just see a huge animal making towards the lake into which it disappeared silently, nor did a ruffle cross the surface of the water. Early the next morning the professor took the skull, and rowing a little way out from the shore flung it as far as possible into the deeper part of the tarn. The werewolf was never seen again.

Here we have a phantom werewolf whose power for evil and ability to materialize in some degree were seemingly energized by the recovery of the skull.

There is a story of a werewolf which was seen by certain shepherds on lonelier hill-sides at night about the middle of the eighteenth century, and there is a tale of a woman who was terribly scared one evening owing to the appearance of a great furry dog with the eyes of a man, which, so far as I can learn, must have been about a hundred years ago, but both of these grow faint with the passing of time. It would not be at all extraordinary if werewolfism survived in the lonelier districts of Wales even at the present day.

It is doubtful whether Holinshed is referring to a werewolf in his *Historie of Scotland*,[50] " Straunge Sightes seene," when he writes : " Also a sort of Woolues in the night season set upon suche as were keeping cattayle abroade in the fieldes and carried away one of them to the woodes, & in the morning suffred him to escape from amongst them againe." In any case he is speaking of a misty and legendary period.

Mr. Elliott O'Donnell gives two examples of werewolfism

in Scotland of comparatively recent years. The one occurred in the Hebrides, and in its details resembles the Merionethshire incident I have just told. The other, which is in some sense more interesting, as relating to a live werewolf and not a phantom, concerns " a mon with evil leerie eyes and eyebrows that met in a point over his nose ", named Saunderson, who dwelled in a cave of Ben MacDhui and who was a known werewolf. His forefathers, too, who had also inhabited the cave, were in their day more than suspect of lupine shape-shifting. As I read, Saunderson would have lived towards the end of the eighteenth century.

To come to an even later date, namely, some ten or at most fifteen years ago, a shepherd who was then occupying a lonely hut in a remoter tract of Inverness-shire, a man described to me as possessing unusually piercing eyes and heavy brows which met so as almost to form an arched bar across the forehead, was commonly reputed to be a werewolf, and certainly the evidence seemed conclusive on this point.

Such cases, however, are rare, and it is clear that even King James, a far more sceptical mind than is vulgarly supposed, had never investigated a case of lycanthropy at first hand, inasmuch as in his *Daemonologie* [51] (1597), the following passage occurs, the interlocutors being Philomathes and Epistemon : " *Phi*. And are not our war-woolfes one sorte of these spirits also, that hauntes and troubles some houses or dwelling-places ?

" *Epi*. There hath indeede bene an old opinion of such like thinges ; For by the *Greekes* they were called λυκανθρωποι, which signifieth men-woolfes. But to tell you simplie my opinion in this, if anie such thing hath bene, I take it to haue proceeded but of a naturall super-abundance of Melancholie, which as wee reade, that it hath made some thinke themselues Pitchers, and some horses, and some one kinde of beast or other. So suppose I that it hath so viciat the imagination and memorie of some, as *per lucida interualla*, it hath so highlie occupyed them, that they haue thought themselues verrie Woolfes indeede at these times ; and so haue counterfeited their actiones in goeing on their handes and feete, preassing to deuoure women and barnes, fighting and snatching with all the towne dogges, and in vsing such like other bruitish actiones, and so to become beastes by a

ENGLAND, WALES, SCOTLAND, IRELAND

stronge apprehension, as *Nebuchad-netzar* was seuen yeares; but as to their hauing and hyding of their hard & schellie sloughes, I take that to be but eiked, by vncertaine report, the author of all lyes."

Nevertheless it was dangerous to accuse anyone of werewolfism. In the Records of the Presbytery of Kelso, 6th November, 1660, a memorial is noted that " Michell Usher, or Wishart, at Sproustoun, and Mausie Ker his wife, complean of John Broun, weaver ther, for calling him a warwoof, and her a witch ".

There is no mention of the metamorphosis into a wolf in such authorities as George Sinclar, *Satans Invisible World Discovered*,[52] Edinburgh, 1685 ; *A History of the Witches of Renfrewshire*, Paisley, 1809 ; Dr. Samuel Hibbert-Ware, *A Description of the Shetland Islands*,[53] 1822 ; Charles Kirkpatrick Sharpe, *A Historical Account of the Belief in Witchcraft in Scotland*,[54] 1820 (1884); Sir Walter Scott, *Letters on Demonology and Witchcraft* (Murray's Family Library), 1830 ; Sir John Graham Dalyell, *The Darker Superstitions of Scotland*,[55] 1834 ; the Rev. John Gregorson Campbell,[56] *Superstitions of the Highlands & Islands of Scotland*, Glasgow, 1900, and *Witchcraft & Second Sight in the Highlands & Islands of Scotland*, Glasgow, 1902 ; H. Drummond Gauld, F.S.A. Scot., *Ghost Tales and Legends*, 1929 ; Alexander Polson, F.S.A. Scot., *Our Highland Folklore Heritage*, Inverness, 1926, and *Scottish Witchcraft Lore*, Inverness, 1932.[57]

With regard to Wales also, neither William Howells, *Cambrian Superstitions*,[58] 1831 ; nor Wirt Sikes, *British Goblins*, 1880 ; nor even the Rev. Elias Owen in his exhaustive study, *Welsh Folk-Lore*,[59] 1896 ; nor Professor John Rhŷs, *Celtic Folklore, Welsh and Manx*,[60] 1901 ; has any mention of werwolfery.

On the other hand, most, if not indeed all, of these writers afford very detailed and considerable evidence concerning the shape-shifting of witches, especially to cats or hares.

Although strictly speaking this metamorphosis, which is generally accomplished by glamour, lies a little outside our province (however nearly akin to it), it cannot be entirely ignored in this connection. I am very well aware that it requires more chapters than I am able to afford pages for a consideration of so important a shape-shifting which should be in any sense deemed adequate or more than a mere touching upon it most lightly in passing.

Gervase of Tilbury writes [61]: " I know from mine own experience that certain women when prowling about at night in the form of cats have been espied by those who were quietly watching in silence and in secret. When these animals have been wounded, upon the very next day the women bear on their bodies in the numerical place the wounds inflicted upon the cat, and if so be a limb has been lopped off the animal, they have lost a corresponsive member." This author, accordingly, fully recognizes the phenomenon of repercussion.

In the *Malleus Maleficarum*,[62] part ii, question i, chapter 9, is related how a workman, living in a certain town of the diocese of Strasburg, was one day chopping wood when he was attacked by three great cats, biting and scratching him. He drove them off with great difficulty, bruising and beating them. To his surprise he was an hour later arrested, and brought before the judge. Nor could he for some days learn the charge since the judge was angry, supposing him to be obstinate in denying the truth. At length he was told he had on such a day at such an hour assaulted three ladies and batooned them so severely they were lying sick abed. Now he knew that was the very time he had driven off the cats, and he revealed the whole matter to the magistrates. Amazed at the event, yet convinced of the sincerity of the man, they realized it was the work of the Devil and dismissed him privily enjoining silence.

Sprenger and Kramer point out that this appearance of the three witches could have happened in two ways. Either the women were converted by glamour into the shape of cats ; or else their three familiars in the likeness of cats attacked the man. In this latter case the blows received by the demons would be instantaneously transferred to the women. Our authors are of opinion that the first method is most likely.

This incident is recorded by several writers as worthy of remark. I find it, for example, in Bodin, *Démonomanie*, livre II, vi ; and in Boguet, *Discours*, c. xlvii.

Bartolomeo Spina in his *Quaestio de Strigibus* [63] holds

LES LUPINS
By Maurice Sand (See p. 237)

[*face p.* 194

ENGLAND, WALES, SCOTLAND, IRELAND

it as certain and proven that by the exercise of black magic and evil glamour witches can and do appear in the shape of cats.

In the year 1566, during the witch-trials of the Evreux district, some terrible and extraordinary evidence was forthcoming. In an old and ancient castle at Vernon [64] a number of sorcerers were wont to assemble for their Sabbat. Four or five rash investigators resolved to watch the proceedings, only to find themselves assailed by a multitude of fierce cats. One of the company was killed by the bites and scratchings of these demoniacal animals, whilst the flesh of the others was shockingly ploughed and torn by their talons. None the less they succeeded in maiming and wounding some of the rout. The next day certain persons long suspect of witchcraft were found to be strangely injured and hurt.[65]

Boguet supplies many instances of this metamorphosis which came under his own experience.[66] One such adventure happened to a man named Charcot of the bailiwick of Gez. Another took place at the Château de Joux, when a traveller wounded a wild cat with his carbine. On arriving at the next inn he found the hostess had just been hurt in the hip by a shot from a carbine.

Paul Sébillot speaks of a sabbat of witches under the glamorous form of cats held in the haunted forest of Bonlieu, and also of two notorious sorceresses, la Dame de Florimont, who lived in the Rossberg (Hautes Vosges) district, and was eventually burned as a witch; and Madame de Badon, of the Château de Marçay, near Chinon, both of whom were adepts in the foul craft of shape-shifting.[67]

In 1875-6 the Rev. Wentworth Webster learned the following in the district of the Labourd : " Witches still appear in the shape of cats, but generally black ones. About two years ago we were told of a man who, at midnight, chopped off the ear of a black cat, who was thus bewitching his cattle, and lo ! in the morning it was a woman's ear, with an earring in it. He deposited it in the Mairie, and we might see it there; but we did not go to look, as it was some distance off." [68]

In English trials for witchcraft the metamorphosis of the accused into a hare or a cat is often brought forward in evidence.[69] One example of each, which shall be chosen from later cases, may be adduced.

At the Summer Assizes held at Taunton before Justice Archer in 1663, Julian Cox, aged about seventy years, was indicted for practising witchcraft. The evidence upon which she was found guilty was overwhelming, but the point that concerns us here is " The first Witness was an Huntsman, who swore that he went out with a pack of Hounds to hunt a Hare, and not far off from *Julian Cox* her house, he at last started a Hare. The *Dogs* hunted her very close, and the third ring hunted her in view, till at last the Huntsman perceiving the Hare almost spent, and making towards a great Bush, he ran on the other side of the Bush to take her up, and preserve her from the Dogs. But as soon as he laid hands on her, it proved to be *Julian Cox*, who had her head groveling on the ground, and her globes (as he exprest it) upward. He knowing her, was affrighted, that his Hair on his Head stood on end ; and yet spake to her, and askt her what brought her there. But she was so far out of Breath, that she could not make him any answer. His Dogs also came up with full cry to recover the game, and smelt at her, and so left off hunting any further. And the Huntsman with his Dogs went home presently, sadly affrighted ".

This account is given by Joseph Glanvil in his *Saducismus Triumphatus*,[70] a work which even so complete an agnostic as W. E. H. Lecky [71] was compelled to acknowledge as— in his own phrase—" probably the ablest book ever published in defence of the superstition," a belief in the supernatural, whilst Glanvil himself, he candidly wrote as philosopher, scholar, and thinker, " has been surpassed in genius by few of his successors."

It does not seem possible that any reasoning and unprejudiced mind should cavil at the evidence of this witness in the trial. It is a plain, straightforward, and essentially veracious statement of fact. Yet, Glanvil remarks, some half-witted people thought he swore false, which *" I suppose was because they imagined that what he told implied that* Julian Cox *was turned into an Hare. Which she was not, nor did his report imply any such real Metamorphosis of her body, but that these ludicrous Dæmons exhibited to the sight of this Huntsman and his Doggs the shape of an Hare, one of them turning himself into such a form, and others hurrying on the body of* Julian *near the same place, and at the same swiftness, but*

ENGLAND, WALES, SCOTLAND, IRELAND

interposing betwixt that Hare-like Spectre and her body, modifying the Air so that the scene there to the beholders sight, was as if nothing but Air were there, and a shew of Earth perpetually suited to that where the Hare passed. As I have heard of some Painters that have drawn the Sky in a huge large Landskip, so lively that the Birds have flown against it, thinking it free Air, and so have fallen down. And if Painters and Juglers by the tricks of Legerdemain can do such strange feats to the deceiving of the sight, it is no wonder that these Airy invisible Spirits as far surpass them in all such præstigious doings as the Air surpasses the Earth for subtilty ".[72]

Glanvil's explanation is interesting and quite admissible. Indeed, it differs only in an unessential detail from the traditional and accepted explanation of glamour, which myself I might perhaps be rather disposed to prefer in this case of the witch Julian Cox.

There is an interesting allusion to the hare-metamorphosis of witches in Matthew Morgan's *Poem Upon the Late Victory over the French Fleet at Sea* (1692) [73] :—

> So Huntsmen think they have a Hare in view,
> And do with eager Cries her Flight pursue.
> But when Sagacious *Jouler* comes so near,
> To seize her hinder Legs and pluck to tear,
> *Comidia* is Couchant in the Thorn,
> And by their half-spent Mouths a Witch is Torn.

One of the latest—although perhaps quite strictly speaking not the very last—of witch-trials in England was the case of Jane Wenham,[74] the " Wise Woman of Walkerne ", who on 4th March, 1711–12, was brought before Mr. Justice Powell at Hertford Assizes. Extraordinary interest had been roused, not only throughout the district but even in London, where the accused became " the discourse of the town ". The evidence proved overwhelming, and in spite of the efforts of Justice Powell, whose attitude showed him to be entirely sceptical, Jane Wenham was formally condemned, only to be reprieved forthwith and soon pardoned.

There were many witnesses, and Anne Thorn, who had been bewitched by Jane Wenham, " saw Things like Cats appear to her " and " always before a Fit she saw a Cat, which would not only appear to her, but speak, and tell her several Things, tempting her to go out of Doors. It was also taken

THE WEREWOLF

notice of that a dismal Noise of Cats was at that Time, and several Times after, heard about the House, sometimes their Cry resembling that of Young Children, at other Times they made a Hellish Noise, to which nothing can be resembled; this was accompany'd by Scratchings, heard by all that were in the House, under the Windows, and at the Doors, which startled and affrighted them all to a great degree; and several People, particularly *James Burvile, Thomas Ireland,* and others, saw these Cats, sometime Three or Four in a Company, which would run to *Jane Wenham*'s House whenever any Body came up to them." Anne Thorn also deposed that " *in the Morning of the 26th of* February, *as she was lying in bed, she saw a Cat sitting in the Window, which spoke to her* ". Naturally in a great fear "*she hid her Head in the Bed-cloathes* ", and presently the cat vanished.

Thomas Ireland was sworn, and deposed " That he hearing a Noise of Cats crying and screaming about the House several Times, went out, and saw several of them, which made towards *Jane Wenham*'s House; that he saw a Cat with a Face like *Jane Wenham* ".

" *James Burvile* was also sworn, who said, That hearing the Scratchings and Noises of Cats, he went out, and saw several of them; that one of them had a Face like *Jane Wenham*." [75]

Various sceptical and agnostic pamphleteers with " plentiful Scatterings of *Billingsgate* Language " soon began to assert " The Impossibility of Witchcraft ", but they were very ably and convincingly answered by Dr. Francis Bragge, who had impartially inquired into the case. As might be expected, Grub Street made a mighty jest of the apparition of a cat which spoke as something " very ridiculous and incredible ", but Dr. Bragge fairly clinches the matter by his answer : " Is it more ridiculous and incredible, that an evil Spirit should assume the Shape of a Cat, and in such a Shape speak so as to be heard and understood, than that the Devil should speak to *Eve* in the Shape of a Serpent ? Which we are oblig'd to believe upon the Credit of Divine Revelation." [76]

I myself have known in my own experience an instance of a witch who assumed the shape of a cat (Oxfordshire), and also a similar metamorphosis into a hare (Devonshire). In both

ENGLAND, WALES, SCOTLAND; IRELAND

cases I make no doubt there was glamour induced by the black art.

In *Memories of Hurstwood, Burnley, Lancashire*,[77] by Tattersall Wilkinson and J. F. Tattersall, is given an interesting account of an old woman, by name Sally Walton, who lived at Cloughfoot Bridge in that district, some forty or fifty years before, and who was reputed a witch. A farmer, who dwelt near, awaking one night saw a large black cat sitting at his feet and watching him intently. Laying hold of a knife which was close at hand the farmer hurled it at the cat, striking one of its fore-legs. The animal vanished, leaving no trace anywhere. The very morning after it was noticed that old Sally had her corresponding arm wrapped in a kerchief, and there was not a neighbour but believed that she had assumed feline shape and visited the farmer's cottage, being wounded by him.

Some cat and hare incidents are recorded by the Rev. W. Henry Jones, of Mumby Vicarage, Alford, in *Lincolnshire Notes and Queries*,[78] October, 1889. A parishioner once told this gentleman that she saw a white rabbit in the churchyard, which being chased into the south porch vanished. At Hogsthorpe there was a hare no dogs could ever catch. One day, passing the house where a reputed witch lived, they heard a great noise, and entering found the old woman being chased about by dogs. The Rev. W. H. Jones' servant from Kirton Lindsey said : " One night my father and brother saw a cat in front of them. Father knew it was a witch and hammered it. Next day the witch had her face all tied up, and shortly afterwards died." " A story of a wizard taking the form of a hare and being slain was told to me a few miles west of Alford." At Grasby a witch who entered a house as a cat was attacked and beaten only to disappear. A little later a woman died, and those who laid out the body saw it was marked just in the same places where the cat had been struck.

Mr. W. Self Weeks, writing in the *Transactions of the Lancashire and Cheshire Antiquarian Society*, vol. xxxiv (1916),[79] relates that he was told by a farmer of Grindleton, near Clitheroe, that a weaver once found a cat near his loom which he in vain tried to drive away. At last in a rage he took a piece of rope and strangled the animal. The next day an old woman long held to be a witch was found dead in her bed. A farmer at Milton related that a few years ago a good house belonging to the Duke of Devonshire, near Bolton Abbey, fell vacant. There were many applicants, and it was eventually let to a man whose family were old tenants of His Grace. He took possession, but was not allowed a moment's peace. When he went to bed he was troubled by bad attacks of nightmare, which he seemed to hear enter his room in spectral form and wellnigh throttle him in a violent grasp. He consulted several doctors who were unable to afford relief, and at last he visited a well-known " wise man " at Leeds. The wise man told him that a certain woman, a neighbour, was at the bottom of the mischief. He was bidden lay a scythe by his bed ready to hand, and when the nightmare seemed to be upon him, to start up and slash at it through the air several times. He followed the instructions implicitly, and was never troubled again. The next morning, however, he heard that a woman who lived near had been taken suddenly and mysteriously ill. She was confined to her bed, and although she lingered many months before she died, she could never walk again. Her name was Hannah H——, an elderly woman, a regular chapel-goer, and esteemed a highly respectable person.

Mrs. Ella Mary Leather, in *The Folk-Lore of Herefordshire*,[80] writes : " Witches can change themselves into the form of animals, usually bats or black cats. A man from Eardisley, going one night to see a neighbour on the Kington Road, whose wife was a reputed witch, met a large black cat at the garden gate. Entering, he asked the man how his wife was. ' Didn't you meet her,' was the answer. ' She has only this minute gone out through the door there ! ' ' So it was certain after that,' my informant added, ' she was a witch, right enough.' . . . At Much Marle (near Ledbury) it was believed that witches became hares in order to lead the foxhounds off the right scent."

The famous Mrs. Anna Eliza Bray, in that most interesting work, *The Tamar and the Tavy*,[81] recounts the story of an old witch, living near Tavistock, who when she needed money would assume the shape of a hare and bid her grandson inform a certain ardent Nimrod who resided hard by

ENGLAND, WALES, SCOTLAND, IRELAND

that a hare was to be found in a given place. The lad was thus always sure to receive a good vail. At length, as the hare could never be caught, suspicion was aroused, and on one occasion when the old woman and her grandson were seen to leave their cottage the hounds were held in readiness to prevent them. The chase was speedier then than the witch cared, and she had only got within her cottage and resumed her shape when the huntsman accompanied by a justice and the parson of the parish were at the door which upon her refusal to open they forced. They found the old hag bleeding, covered with wounds, and still panting, hard breathed. She denied she had cozened them in the shape of a hare, but when they threatened to call in the pack she confessed her sorceries.

With regard to Scotland, I have collected a not inconsiderable amount of evidence, some from oral sources, but this must be reserved for a special study of the subject. At the present it will suffice to refer to the instances given by the Rev. J. G. Campbell in his *Witchcraft & Second Sight in the Highlands & Islands of Scotland*, to which study attention has already been drawn. He mentions the various forms in which the warlock may be disguised—ravens, rats, mice, black sheep, " and very frequently cats and hares." " The stories of witches assuming the shape of hares are numberless. . . . When a witch assumes this shape it is dangerous to fire at her without putting silver, a sixpence or a button of that metal, in the gun. If the hare fired at was, as indeed it often was, a witch in disguise, the gun burst, and the shot came back and killed the party firing, or some mischance followed. Old women used, therefore, to recommend that a sixpence be put in the gun when firing at a hare." [82]

A very remarkable account is given in Charles St. John's *Wild Sports and Natural History of the Highlands* [83] of the tranvection of a witch " possessed of more than mortal power ". After having long plagued the countryside with her sorceries she is said to have been brought down one night as she skirled through the air by a pot-valiant old soldier who loaded his gun with a double charge of powder and in place of shot a crooked sixpence and some silver buttons. Well-lined with whisky he fired when he saw her " just coming like a muckle bird right towards him ". In the morning he was found lying half-asleep and half in a swoon, his gun burst beside him, and a fine large heron shot through and through on the ground, " which heron as everyone felt assured was the cailleach herself ". The place where this happened is a bleak cold-looking piece of water known as Lochan-na-cailleaich (the witch's tarn), and Donald the beater who told the story added : " her ghaist is still to the fore, and the loch side is no canny after the gloaming." Allowing for natural exaggeration there is certainly a true story here.

W. N. Neil, in a study *Witch-Cats in Scotland*,[84] remarks : " The murderous ferocity of these Highland witch-cats compared to the milder nature of their sisters in the Lowlands almost leads one to think that it was not the common domestic cat that was the therianthropic shape chosen by the northern witches, but that of the spitting, swearing, untameable wild-cat which is a prominent representative of the Highland fauna to this day. The same conjecture may also explain the absence of the true werwolf from Scottish story, although the actual wolves persisted in its mountains and its moors till the eve of the Battle of Culloden. The wild-cat being comparatively common and noted for its cruelty and ferocity would be a far more suitable disguise for a witch than a sporadic and possibly timid wolf." The timidity of the wolf may be questioned.

The Rev. Elias Owen, in his *Welsh Folk-Lore*, to which reference has already been made, gives a large number of instances of witches transforming themselves into cats or hares. One example of each must briefly suffice. On the road between Cerrigydrudion and Bettws-y-Coed stood an inn kept by two women, sisters, of prepossessing manners and appearance, which, however, acquired an ill-name owing to the mysterious robberies that occurred in the house, although travellers confessed that the doors of their rooms always remained locked in the morning just as they had fastened them the night before. The parson of Llan Festiniog [85] resolved to unravel the business. Accordingly he obtained a lodging at the hostelry, but on going to bed kept a candle burning in the room. As he feigned sleep two cats stealthily crept through a narrow partition, and approaching his clothes seemed to fumble them with their

ENGLAND, WALES, SCOTLAND, IRELAND

paws as though feeling for his purse. Like lightning he struck with his sword and amid terrible screams the animals disappeared. Next morning only one of the sisters waited on him, and he was informed the other sister was indisposed. However, he forced his way to her presence and found that her right hand was bandaged just where he had wounded the cat. He then revealed who he was, and solemnly exhorted them to abandon their shape-shifting and sorceries.

The following incident happened to the Rector of Llanycil a few years before *Welsh Folk-Lore* was written, and is therefore an entirely modern example. When his servant was churning milk it was found that in spite of her efforts the milk would not churn. Upon removing the lid, however, out leaped a huge hare and ran off at full speed, whereupon the milk came easily enough. A wise man in Wales said that a witch in the shape of a hare could only be caught by a black greyhound. Mr. Owen also notes the unlucky omen of a hare crossing the path, and gives an interesting example.

C. I. Elton, in his *Origins of English History*,[86] writes that " The oldest Welsh laws contain several allusions to the magical character of the hare which was thought to change its sex every month or year, and to be the companion of witches who often assumed its shape ". In Western Brittany hares are much feared. Essex Smith, in his *Fairies and Witches in Old Radnorshire*,[87] has several examples of hare and cat transformations. " Witches in the form of hares were numerous in Radnorshire. One huge hare, grey with extreme age, lived on Clyro Hill for many years; she could neither be shot nor caught with harriers or greyhounds; and was believed by all the countryside to be a witch. She had her regular rounds, and every morning early she came and sat under a bush near Tynessa."

The Manx witches are known as *butches*, which is probably nothing more than a variant of the English word. They are credited with the power of shape-shifting and their especial metamorphosis is that of the hare, when they are so fleet that only a black greyhound can catch them, and no shot save it be silver can hurt them. In Wales, generally speaking, only women can appear as hares, but in the Manx tradition both men and women assume this shape. This property is also said to run in certain families, and Professor

Rhŷs in his *Celtic Folklore* [88] mentions a smith in the neighbourhood of Ramsey who was known as *gaaue mwaagh* " the hare smith ". A witch if wounded as a hare resumes the human shape and the spell is broken, but the hurt always remains.

The cat-transformation is known in the Channel Islands, and here also werewolfery was once rife, but the tradition wanes. Sir Edgar MacCulloch in his *Guernsey Folk Lore*,[89] a book of the deepest interest, says : " The ' Varou ', now almost entirely forgotten, seems to have belonged to the family of nocturnal goblins. He is allied to the ' Loup-Garou ' of the French, and the ' Were-Wolf ' of the English, if, indeed, he is not absolutely identical with them. He is believed to be endowed with a marvellous appetite, and it is still proverbially said of a great eater ' Il mange comme un varou '.

" ' Aller en varouverie ' was an expression used in former times in speaking of those persons who met together in unfrequented places for the purposes of debauchery or other illicit practices. Thus one night such a one was heard saying that the time was propitious ' pour aller en varouverie sous l'épine '. *Varou* was originally from the Breton *Varw*— ' the dead '—and was identified with the ' Heroes ' or beatified warriors who were, by Homer and Hesiod, supposed to be in attendance on Saturn. Guernsey, in the days of Demetrius, was known by the name of the Isle of Heroes, or of Demons, and Saturn was said to be confined there in a ' golden rock ' bound by ' golden chains '."

In Guernsey the word *varou* still lingers in place-names. The " Creux des Varous " is a subterranean cavern, which extends, folk say, from Houmet to L'Erée ; a plot of ground near the cromlech of L'Erée (" Le Creux des Fées ") is still known as " Le Camp du Varou ", and an estate in the parish of S. Saviour is called " Le Mont-Varou ". " Old people still remember that it used to be said in their youth that ' Le Char des Varous ' was to be heard rolling over the cliffs and rocks on silver-tyred wheels, between Houmet and the Castle of Albecq, before the death of any of the great ones of the earth ; and how this supernatural warning was sure to be followed almost immediately by violent storms and tempests."

" Sorcerers have the power of taking the forms of different

ENGLAND, WALES, SCOTLAND, IRELAND

animals, but when thus disguised cannot be wounded but by silver.

" A Mr. Le Marchant, ' des grent mesons,' had often fired at a white rabbit which frequented his warren, but without success. One day, however, beginning to suspect how the case really stood, he detached his silver sleeve-button from his wrist-band, loaded his gun with it, took a steady aim, and fired. The rabbit immediately disappeared behind the hedge. He ran up, and, hearing some person groaning as if in great pain on the other side, looked over and recognized a neighbour of his, a lady of the Vale, who was lying with her leg broken and bleeding profusely from a fresh wound."

The evidence for werewolfism in Ireland is of immemorial antiquity and persists through the centuries. Lycanthropy was believed for the most part to run in families, and an early tradition in the *Cóir Anmann* (*Fitness of Names*) has : " Laignech *Fáelad*, that is, he was the man that used to shift into *fáelad*, i.e. wolf-shapes. He and his offspring after him used to go, whenever they pleased, into the shapes of the wolves, and, after the custom of wolves, kill the herds. Wherefore he was called Laignech *Fáelad*, for he was the first of them (the group composed of Laignech and his descendants) to go into a wolf-shape." [90] This was in Ossory.[91]

From the *Leabhar Na H-Uidhri* (*The Book of the dun Cow*),[92] the oldest volume now known entirely in the Irish language, we learn that the Druids practised the magic art of shapeshifting.

An old Irish legend, which is given in *Kongs Skuggsjo* (*Speculum Regale*), a Norse book compiled about 1250, runs as follows : " There is also in that land (Ireland) one wonderful thing, which will seem very untruthful to men. Yet the people who inhabit that land say that it is certainly true. And that befell on account of the wrath of a holy man. It is said that when the holy Patricius was preaching Christianity in that land, there was one great race more hostile to him than the other people that were in the land. And these men tried to do him many kinds of injury. And when he preached Christianity to them as to other men, and came to meet them when they were holding their assembly, then they took this counsel, to howl at him like wolves.

But when he saw that his message would succeed little with these people, then he became very wroth, and prayed God that He might avenge it on them by some judgement, that their descendants might for ever remember their disobedience. And great punishment and fit and very wonderful has since befallen their descendants; for it is said that all men who come from that race are always wolves at a certain time, and run into the woods and take food like wolves; and they are worse in this that they have human reason, for all their cunning, and such desire and greed for men as for other creatures. And it is said that some become so every seventh year, and are men during the interval. And some have it so long that they have seven years at once, and are never so afterwards." [93]

I do not find this in the life of S. Patrick and the account of this Saint given by the Bollandists, under 17th March,[94] although one might have expected to meet with it in chapter xiii of the *Vita S. Patricii* by the Cistercian Jocelyn of Furness (*fl.* 1200), which has rubric *Patricio resistentes seuere castigantur.* Neither is the incident mentioned in the *Tripartite Life of S. Patrick*, but among the miracles of the Saint is recorded " Coroticus King of the Britons [changed] into the shape of a fox in his country ".[95]

In the *Book of Ballymote*,[96] a miscellaneous collection embracing historical, legendary, genealogical, and other matter, some of which is very ancient, compiled about the beginning of the fifteenth century, a passage says that " the children of the wolf " in Ossory could transform themselves and go abroad to devour people.

A Latin hexameter poem of the thirteenth century on the *Wonders of Ireland*, printed by Thomas Wright and J. O. Halliwell in their *Reliquiae Antiquae*,[97] has fourteen lines *De hominibus qui se uertunt in lupos*, which run : " There are certain men of the Celtic race who have a marvellous power which comes to them from their forbears. For by an evil craft they can at will change themselves into the shape of wolves with sharp tearing teeth, and often thus transformed will they fall upon poor defenceless sheep, but when folk armed with clubs and weapons run to attack them shouting lustily then do they flee and scour away apace. Now when they are minded to transform themselves they leave their

ENGLAND, WALES, SCOTLAND, IRELAND

own bodies, straitly charging their friends neither to move or touch them at all, however lightly, for if this be done never will they be able to return to their human shape again. If whilst they are wolves anyone hurts or wounds them, then upon their own bodies the exact wound or mark can plainly be seen. And with much amaze have they been espied in human form with great gobbets of raw bleeding flesh champed in their jaws." The same account, commencing "The descendants of the Wolf are in Ossory", is given in the Irish version (MS. D) of the *Historia Britonum* of Nennius of Bangor.[98]

Giraldus Cambrensis, in his *Topographia Hibernica*,[99] Distinctio ii, cap. 19, has the following account of werewolfery: " About three years before the arrival of Prince John in Ireland,[100] it chanced that a certain priest, who was journeying from Ulster towards Meath, was benighted in a wood that lies on the boundures of Meath. Whilst he, and the young lad his companion, were watching by a fire they had kindled under the leafy branches of a large tree, there came up to them a wolf who immediately addressed them in the following words: 'Do not alarm yourselves and do not be in any way afraid. You need not fear, I say, where there is no reason for fear.' The travellers none the less were thrown in a great damp and were astonied. But the wolf reverently called upon the Name of God. The priest then adjured him, straitly charging him by Almighty God and in the might of the Most Holy Trinity that he should do them no sort of harm, but rather tell them what sort of creature he was who spake with a human voice. The wolf replied with seemly speech, and said: 'In number we are two, to wit a man and a woman, natives of Ossory, and every seven years on account of the curse laid upon our folk by the blessed Abbot S. Natalis,[101] a brace of us are compelled to throw off the human form and appear in the shape of wolves. At the end of seven years, if perchance these two survive they are able to return again to their homes, reassuming the bodies of men, and another two must needs take their place. Howbeit my wife, who labours with me under this sore visitation, lies not far from hence, grievously sick. Wherefore I beseech you of your good charity to comfort her with the aid of your priestly office.'

When he had so said, the wolf led the way to a tree at no great distance, and the priest followed him trembling at the strangeness of the thing. In the hollow of the tree he beheld a wolfen,[102] and she was groaning piteously mingled with sad human sighs. Now when she saw the priest she thanked him very courteously and gave praise to God Who had vouchsafed her such consolation in her hour of utmost need.

"The priest then shrived her and gave her all the last rites of Holy Church so far as the houselling. Most earnestly did she entreat him that she might receive her God, and that he would administer to her the crown of all, the Body of the Lord.

"The priest, however, declared that he was not provided with the holy viaticum, when the man-wolf, who had withdrawn apart for a while, came forward and pointed to the wallet, containing a mass-book and some consecrated Hosts which, according to the use of his country, the good priest was carrying suspended from his neck under his clothing. The man-wolf entreated him not to deny them any longer the Gift of God, which it was not to be questioned, Divine Providence had sent to them. Moreover to remove all doubt, using his claw as a hand, he drew off the pelt from the head of the wolfen and folded it back even as far down as the navel, whereupon there was plainly to be seen the body of an old woman. Upon this the priest, since she so instantly besought him, urged though it may be more by fear than by reasoning, hesitated no longer but gave her Holy Communion, which she received most devoutly from his hands. Immediately after this the man-wolf rolled back the skin again, fitting it to its former place.

"These holy rites having been duly rather than regularly performed, the man-wolf joined their company by the fire they had kindled under the tree and showed himself a human being not a four-footed beast. In the early morning, at cock-light he led them safely out of the wood, and when he left them to pursue their journey he pointed out to them the best and shortest road, giving them directions for a long way. In taking leave also, he thanked the priest most gratefully and in good set phrase for the surpassing kindness he had shown, promising moreover that if it were God's will he should return home (and already two parts of the

ENGLAND, WALES, SCOTLAND, IRELAND

period during which he was under the malediction had passed) he would take occasion to give further proofs of his gratitude.

"As they were parting the priest inquired of the man-wolf whether the enemy (the English invader) who had now landed on their shores would continue long to possess the land. The wolf replied : 'On account of the sins of our nation and their enormous wickedness the anger of God, falling upon an evil generation, hath delivered them into the hands of their enemies. Therefore so long as this foreign people shall walk in the way of the Lord and keep His commandments, they shall be safe and not to be subdued ; but if—and easy is the downward path to iniquity and nature prone to evil—it come to pass that through dwelling among us they turn to our whoredoms, then assuredly will they provoke the wrath of the Lord upon themselves also.'

"It so happened that about two years later when I was passing through Meath, the Bishop of that diocese had summoned a synod, and had requested the honourable attendance of the Bishops of neighbouring sees and my Lords the Abbots, in order that they might take counsel together concerning this incident which the priest had related to him. The Bishop, learning that I was travelling in those parts, sent two of his priests to me, asking me if it were possible to attend the synod at which a matter of such grave importance was to be deliberated, and, if indeed I could not assist in person, he begged me at least to give them my opinion and judgement in writing. When I had heard the whole circumstance in detail from the two priests (although indeed I had been told of it before by many others), inasmuch as I was prevented by many weighty affairs from attending the synod, I was fain amend for my absence by giving my advice in a letter. The Bishop and the full synod so far approved of my counsel, that they followed it forthwith, commanding the priest to travel to Rome, and there to lay the whole thing before the Holy Father,[103] delivering to him letters containing the priest's own account, which was certified by the seals of all the Bishops and Abbots who had been present at the conclave.

"It is not to be disputed, but must be most certainly believed that for our salvation the Divine Nature assumed human nature. Now in the present case we find that at God's bidding in order to manifest His supreme power and righteousness by a very miracle human nature assumed the form of a wolf.

"The point arises: Was this creature man or beast? A rational animal is far above the level of a brute beast. Are we to class in the species man a four-footed animal, whose face is bent to the earth, and who cannot indulge in the visible faculty? Would he who slew this animal be a murderer? We reply that the miracles of God are not to be made the subjects of argument and human disputation, but are to be wondered at in all humility."

Giraldus, having come to this very admirable and sane conclusion, then discusses the famous passages in S. Augustine, *De Ciuitate Dei*, xvi, 8, and xviii, 17 and 18.

He sums up: "In our own day also we have seen persons, who deeply skilled in magic arts, turned any substance which was of sufficient quantity into fat porkers as they seemed (but curiously they were always of a reddish hue), and these they sold in the markets. None the less the glamour vanished as soon as they crossed any water and the substance returned to its true material form. However carefully they were kept, they could not retain their spurious appearance more than three days.

"It is commonly known, and has been bitterly complained of in former days as well as now, that certain foul hags in Wales, as well as in Ireland and Scotland, change themselves into the shape of hares, and under this counterfeit form sucking the teats of cows they secretly rob other persons of their milk.

"We hold then with S. Augustine that neither demons nor sorcerers can either create or essentially change their natures; but those, whom God has created are able by His permission to metamorphize themselves so far as mere outward appearance is concerned, so that they appear to be what truly they are not, and the senses of men beholding them are fascinated and deceived by glamour, so that things are not seen as they really exist, but by some phantom power or magic spell the human vision is deluded and mocked inasmuch as it rests upon unreal and fictitious forms."

Camden,[104] writing of Wolf-men in Tipperary, says: "Whereas some of the Irish and such as would be thought worthy of credit, doe affirme, that certaine men in this

ENGLAND, WALES, SCOTLAND, IRELAND

tract are yeerely turned into Wolves; surely I suppose it be a meere fable: unlesse happly through that malicious humour of predominant unkind Melancholie, they be possessed with the malady that the Phisitians call Λυκανθρωπία, which raiseth and engendreth such like phantasies, as that they imagine themselves to be transformed into Wolves. Neither dare I otherwise affirme of these metamorphised *Lycaones* in *Liveland*, concerning whom many writers deliver many and meruailous reports."

Sir William Temple, in his essay *Of Poetry*,[105] commenting upon "those Trophies of Enchantment . . . Productions of the *Gothick Wit* . . . all the visionary Tribe of *Fairies, Elves*, and *Goblins*, of *Sprites* and *Bulbeggars* ", continues: " How much of this Kind, and of this Credulity remained even to our own Age, may be observed by any Man that reflects so far as thirty or forty Years; how often avouched, and how generally credited, were the Stories of *Fairies, Sprites, Witchcrafts*, and *Enchantments?* In some Parts of *France*, and not longer ago, the common People believed certainly there were *Lougaroos*, or Men turned into Wolves; and I remember several *Irish* of the same Mind."

---

[1] A note by Sir Simon Degge, who was born in 1612 and lived to the age of 92. This note is printed in the Rev. Thomas Harwood's edition (1820) of Sampson Eredeswick's *Survey of Staffordshire*, pp. 2 and 3.

[2] Robertson, *Buxton and the Peak*, p. 41, quoted by Harting.

[3] The authoritative study is *British Animals Extinct within Historic Times*, by James Edmund Harting, F.L.S., F.Z.S., London, Trübner, 1880, an admirable work from which I have not hesitated to draw freely for details of the wolf in Great Britain and Ireland. Harting emphasizes (p. 204) that " in order to confine the subject within reasonable limits " he carefully abstains from any mention of the werewolf or wolf-legends. If I give any quotation from Harting, and not from the original source, I have been careful to mention this in the corresponsive note.

[4] *The Original Chronicle of Andrew of Wyntoun*, ed. F. J. Amours, The Scottish Text Society, vol. ii, p. 312 (Wemyss MS.), ch. xxxix, ll. 617–622.

[5] Antwerp, 1605, p. 59.

[6] Migne, *Patres Latini*, lxxxix, column 426, D. The *Poenitentiale* is now generally considered to be a Frankish compilation of the ninth century and largely drawn from Halitgar. See H. J. Schmitz, *Die Bussbücher und die Bussdisciplin der Kirche*, Mainz, 1883, Theil iii, Kapitel 4, " Poenitentiale Egberti," pp. 565–587.

[7] *Britannia. Britain* . . . " Written first in Latine by *William Camden*, Clarenceux K. of A. Translated newly into English by *Philemon Holland* . . . Finally revised . . . by the said Author." Folio, Londini, 1610, Yorke-shire, p. 715.

⁸ Raphael Holinshed, *The Firste volume of the Chronicles of England, Scotlande, and Irelande*, 1577 ; The Thirde Booke, cap. 7, "Of sauuage beastes and vermines," p. 108. Holinshed claims that England is " void of noysome beasts, as Lions, Beares, Tygers, Wolfes, and such like : by meanes whereof our countrymen may trauaile in safetie ". Which cannot be said to-day.
⁹ Folio, 1612, p. 135.
¹⁰ Ibid., p. 144. Selden quotes as his authority : *Itin. Leicest.* 27. Hen. 3. *in Archiu. Turr.* Londin.
¹¹ 4to, 1677. Term Catalogues, Hilary, 28th February, 1678.
¹² 4to, 1678. Term Catalogues, Michaelmas, 26th November, 1677.
¹³ 4to, 1735. Book the Third, ll. 13–19 ; pp. 50–1.
¹⁴ Joannis Caii Britanni *de Canibus Britannis.* Liber Unus. Londini, per Gulielmum Seresium. 8vo, 1570. I have used the edition in *The Works of John Caius, M.D.,* ed. John Venn and E. S. Roberts, Cambridge, 1912, p. 10 (*De Canibus*), and quote the English version *Of Englishe Dogges,* by Abraham Fleming, 1576, as there reprinted, pp. 21 and 22 of the *Treatise.* Thomas Pennant, *Tours in Wales,* 1778–1781 (new edition, by Professor Rhŷs, 3 vols., 1883), remarks that "the report of *Edgar's* having extirpated the race of wolves out of the principality, is erroneous," vol. i (1883), p. 113.
¹⁵ *Monumenta Historica Britannica,* vol. i, pp. 856–872, *De Bello Hastingensi Carmen,* ll. 571–2 ; p. 867. Guy was Bishop of Amiens 1059 to 1075.
¹⁶ Harl. MSS., No. 3859, ed. Williams, Rolls Series, pp. 50–1. " Apud Kermerden lupus rabiosus duo de uiginti homines momordit qui omnes fere protinus perierunt." The MS. is believed to be a translation from the original Welsh.
¹⁷ It is said that the story of Gellert is found in many literatures. It certainly resembles the tale of the Knight and his Greyhound in *The Seven Wise Masters.* See further, Heinrich Adelbert von Keller, *Li romans des sept sages,* Tübingen, 1830, p. clxxviii. William Robert Spencer's poem, *Beth-Gêlert, or The Grave of the Greyhound,* signed Dôlymelynllyn, 11th August, 1800, was privately printed (4 pp.) by Collingwood, Oxford, but not published. *Beth-Gêlert* was first published in *Poems* (pp. 78–86) by William Robert Spencer, London, Cadell and Davies, 1811.
¹⁸ I have used the facsimile edition with introduction by William Blades, London, Elliot Stock, 1881. The allusion to Tristram is to Sir Tristram of the Table Round, who was a mighty hunter and a great authority on all matters of venery. He was popularly supposed to have been the author of many (if not all) hunting terms, and his name was constantly invoked to clench a statement, as it were.
¹⁹ *The Noble Arte of Venerie or Hunting,* 4to, 1575, chapters 75 and 76. The pages are wrongly numbered, 363 and 362 ; followed by p. 205 to p. 214. Turbervile gives two chapters to hunting the wolf.
²⁰ *Heir beginnis the hystory and croniklis of Scotland.* John Bellenden's translation of Boece. Edinburgh, 1541. Ca. xi, " of the gret plente of haris, hartis, and vthir vvild bestiall in Scotland." Sig. C. ii.
²¹ Trans. Philemon Holland, ut cit. sup., *Scotia, Scotland,* p. 54.
²² There are, of course, various stories concerning the killing of the last wolf who infested a certain district in Scotland, as for example the last wolf killed at Lochaber by Sir Ewen Cameron in 1680, which Pennant misunderstood to be the last wolf killed in Scotland : *British Zoology,* vol. i, p. 88, and *Tour in Scotland,* vol. i, p. 206. Surtees, *History and Antiquities of the County of Durham,* vol. ii, p. 172, gives 1682 as the date of the killing of the last wolf in Scotland. Sir Thomas Dick Lauder in his *Account of the Moray Floods of August, 1829,* relates how MacQueen of Pall-à-chrocain slew the last wolf, but says that the scene of this exploit was in the parish of Moy, county Inverness. He also has another story of two old wolves and their cubs being killed at Knoch of Braemory, near the source of the Burn of Newton.
²³ Holinshed, op. cit., p. 9 ; Camden, op. cit., *Ireland,* p. 63. Cf. from MS. Rawl. B. 512 : " As Paradise is without beasts, without a snake, without a lion, without a dragon, without a scorpion, without a mouse, without a

ENGLAND, WALES, SCOTLAND, IRELAND

frog, so is Ireland in the same manner without any harmful animal, save only the wolf, as sages say." *Tripartite Life of S. Patrick*, ed. W. Stokes, Rolls Series, part i (1887), p. xxx.

[24] "Translated from the Italian Manuscript in the Laurentian Library at Florence," London, 1821, p. 108.

[25] p. 854. This article was afterwards incorporated by the author in his *The Dog: its Origin, Natural History, and Varieties*, 1848. My reference to *The Irish Penny Journal* is from Harting, p. 202. In *A Brief Character of Ireland*, 12mo, 1692 (Licensed 16th Nov., 1691), a stupid enough squib, the peasants of remoter districts are described as "like their Native Wolves", p. 47.

[26] London, 1882 : p. 149, p. 228, and p. 3.

[27] Herm. Jos. Schmitz, *Die Bussbücher und das Kanonische Bussverfahren*, ii Band, "Die Bussbücher und die Bussdisciplin der Kirche," Düsseldorf, 1898, p. 442.

[28] Variants are : weruvolff, Werewolf, werwolf, Werewl., and wertvoos.

[29] "Liber poenitentialis . . . per magistrum Bartholomaeum Exoniensem episcopum collectus . . ." British Museum, Cotton MSS., Faust. A. viii ; 1.

[30] See Chapter I, n. 18.

[31] *Otia Imperialia*, ed. Felix Liebrecht, Hanover, 1856, pp. 51–2.

[32] Titulus, LVIII, i. *Recueil des Historiens des Gaules et de la France*, Paris, 1741, ed. Dom Martin Bouquet, O.S.B. (Maurist). Tom. iv, p. 154.

[33] Frédéric Pluquet, *Contes Populaires*, Rouen, 1834, 2me édition, "Le Loup-garou," p. 15.

[34] Benjamin Thorpe, *Ancient Laws and Institutes of England*, 1840, vol. i, p. 445.

[35] Ibid., p. 591. Henrici Primi, lxxxiii, 5. The Laws of Henry I are now generally regarded as a twelfth-century compilation with a generic title.

[36] To be dated c. 1400. *Gamelyn*, 700–1. Chaucer, ed. W. W. Skeat, Oxford, 1894 ; vol. iv, *Canterbury Tales*, text. Appendix to Group A, p. 662. John Urry died 1715, and his edition of Chaucer was published posthumously in 1721. Tyrwhitt's *Canterbury Tales* was issued 4 vols., 1775 ; a fifth volume followed in 1778.

[37] No. xxi, ed. England and Pollard, *Early English Text Society*, 1897, p. 232, l. 139. See also Lydgate, *Bochas*, vii, 1261.

[38] Ed. F. W. D. Brie, *E. E. Text Soc.*, 1906, part i, pp. 169–170.

[39] Walter of Hemingburgh, *Chronicon*, ed. H. C. Hamilton, London, 1848 ; vol. i, pp. 252–4.

[40] *The Dramatic Writings of John Bale*, edited by J. S. Farmer. Early English Dramatists, 1907. *King Johan* has been edited separately by J. H. P. Pafford, 1931.

[41] In two parts, 4to, 1591.

[42] It is, of course, true that in *King John*, Act V, scene 6, Hubert cries :—
   The King I fear is poyson'd by a Monke, . . .
   A Monke I tell you, a resolued villaine
   Whose Bowels sodainly burst out :
and in the following scene the "fell poison" is spoken of, whilst the King himself exclaims : "Poyson'd, ill fare." But previous to all this on the battle-field, v, 3, King John had groaned :—
   Aye me, this tyrant Feauer burnes mee vp, . . .
   Weaknesse possesseth me, and I am faint.
The Troublesome Raigne of King John is gutter Protestantism, and as such of no account. Bowden in his *Religion of Shakespeare* (p. 120) acutely observes : "Shakespeare, in adapting it, had only to leave untouched its virulent bigotry and its ribald stories of friars and nuns to secure its popularity, yet as a fact he carefully excludes the anti-catholic passages and allusions, and acts throughout as a rigid censor on behalf of the Church." J. P. Chesney, *Shakespeare as a Physician*, 1884, comments on the cry "Poyson'd, ill fare" that "the case of King John bears a much closer analogy to a case wherein the hand of nature has been instrumental in saturating the system with poison, than it does to one in which a 'villainous Monk' had been the

instrument. Miasmatic exhalations had no doubt wrought the evil in this case ".

[43] " Coram altari magno in medio inter sacrosancta corpora Oswaldi et Vulfstani, pontificum beatorum." Nicolas Trivet O.P., *Annales*, ed. T. Hog, London, 1845, p. 197.

[44] Roger of Wendover, iii, 385.

[45] " Sepultus, dico, est, sed non cum honore regio, quia terra quae in operibus suis pessimis turbata extitit nondum ad plenum pacificata quieuit." Ed. cit., p. 254. Walter of Hemingburgh has a story of King John appearing " in uestibus quasi deauratis " and all fulgent with light to a certain priest, but he obviously doubts the tale, and indeed the vision may have been a diabolic illusion, although, as we hope, he was saved by the intercession of S. Wulstan.

[46] See Gabriel de Moulin, Curé de Maneual, *Histoire générale de Normandie*, livre XIV, xxxiii, Rouen, folio, 1631, p. 559.

[47] Amélie Bosquet, *La Normandie romanesque et merveilleuse*, Paris, 1845, chap. xii, p. 238.

[48] *Werwolves*, London, 1912, chapter vi, pp. 92–109.

[49] This is, I think, the same incident as was told by Mr. J. Wentworth Day in *The Passing Show*, 9th July, 1932, " Exploring the Uncanny—No. 4. The Terror on the Mountain," pp. 24–5. Mr. Day also mentions the werewolf seen by the shepherds, and the incident of the woman scared by the great dog with the eyes of a man.

[50] Ed. cit., pp. 40–1.

[51] Third Booke, chap. i, edited by G. B. Harrison, " The Bodley Head Quartos," 1924, pp. 61–2.

[52] I have used the reprint by Thomas George Stevenson, Edinburgh, 1871.

[53] " Witchcraft of Shetland," pp. 572–584, and notes, pp. 592–601.

[54] For which see Bibliography.

[55] It should perhaps be mentioned that the same author's *Rare and Remarkable Animals of Scotland*, 2 vols., London, 1848, deals with animal products resembling flowers, or shrubs, or trees, and " with other foliaceous products " (vol. ii, chapter i, p. 1) and various zoophytes, but does not treat of any quadrupeds.

[56] The Rev. John Gregorson Campbell was minister of Tiree 1861–1891, and the collections in his two books were especially valuable in that they were " Collected entirely from Oral Sources ". In his *Witchcraft and Second Sight*, pp. 30–44, he deals with witches as sheep, hares, cats, rats, gulls, cormorants, whales.

[57] The Scotch and Welsh folklore contained in Κρυπτάδια, " Recueil de documents pour servir à l'étude des Traditions populaires," vol. ii, Heilbronn, 1884, although valuable, is almost entirely of an erotic nature and has no mention of werewolfery. This is also the case with the French, Polish, and Russian collections given in vol. v (Paris, 1898) of the same series.

[58] William Howells, the son of the Rev. J. Howells, vicar of Tipton, was only eighteen at the time he wrote this book.

[59] *Welsh Folk-Lore*, by the Rev. Elias Owen, M.A., F.S.A., of Llanyblodwel. Oswestry and Wrexham, 1906, pp. 224–233.

[60] 2 vols., Oxford, 1901 ; vol. i, pp. 293–6.

[61] *Otia Imperialia*, Tertia Decisio, xciii, ed. cit., p. 45.

[62] Eng. tr., ut cit. sup., pp. 126–7.

[63] 4to, Romae, 1576, cap. xix : " Experientiae apparentis conuersionis strigum in catos."

[64] Vernon on the Eure is some 25 kilometres from Evreux. The castle is of the thirteenth century. See Th. Michel, *Histoire de la ville et du canton de Vernon*, 1851 ; and E. Mayer, *Histoire de la ville de Vernon*, 2 vols., 1875–7.

[65] Bodin, *Demonomanie*, Liv. ii, ch. vi. See a note by M. F. Bourquelot, *Recherches sur la Lycanthropie* : *Mémoires de la Soc. des Antiquaires de France*, tome xix (N. Série, tom. ix), Paris, 1849, pp. 246–7. Also Paul Sébillot, *Le Folk-Lore de France*, tom. iv, Paris, 1907, p. 195.

[66] *Discours des Sorciers*, 1590, ch. xlvii. Eng. tr. *Examen of Witches*, 1929, p. 142.

ENGLAND, WALES, SCOTLAND, IRELAND

[67] Sébillot, op. cit., tom. i, p. 281, and tom. iv, pp. 304–5.
[68] *Basque Legends*, second ed., 1879, p. 70 n. The first edition is 1877.
[69] The shape-shifting of a witch is, of course, an entirely different thing from the appearance of a familiar in animal guise. None the less, Mr. G. L. Kittredge has persistently confused the two, and in consequence his chapter "Metamorphosis" (*Witchcraft in Old and New England*, 1928, pp. 174–184) presents an entanglement not a little difficult to unravel.
[70] London, 1681, the Second Part, Relation viii, pp. 190–1.
[71] *History of the Rise and Influence of the Spirit of Rationalism in Europe*, 2 vols., 1865 ; vol. i, p. 126, and p. 120.
[72] Ed. cit., Relation viii, p. 200.
[73] 4to, 1692, p. 18. For *Comidia* we should surely read *Canidia*.
[74] See Montague Summers, *The Geography of Witchcraft*, 1927, ch. ii, pp. 158–160.
[75] *A Full and Impartial Account of the Discovery of Sorcery and Witchcraft Practis'd by Jane Wenham of Walkerne in Hertfordshire . . . Also Her Tryal . . .* London, 1712, pp. 17, 23, 29.
[76] *Witchcraft Farther Display'd*, London, 1712, p. 38. Introduction signed F[rancis] B[ragge], *Ardely-Bury, April* the 3d, 1712. He remarks that even " while she is in Prison " the " wicked old Witch " Mother Wenham, " has found out a Way to get plenty of Money."
[77] 1889, pp. 57–8.
[78] Vol. i, part 8, pp. 244–9.
[79] Manchester, 1917, pp. 104–6.
[80] Hereford, 1912 ; " Witchcraft," p. 52.
[81] *A Description of the Part of Devonshire bordering on the Tamar and the Tavy*, 3 vols., London, 1836, vol. ii, pp. 277–9. For parallels to this story see Rev. Elias Owen, *Welsh Folk-Lore*, 1896, pp. 230–3, and Mrs. Ella Mary Leather, *The Folk-Lore of Herefordshire*, 1912, p. 52.
[82] Op. cit., pp. 6–8.
[83] Edited by the Rt. Hon. Sir Herbert Maxwell, Bt., London and Edinburgh, 1919, pp. 37–9. Charles St. John died in July, 1856.
[84] *The Occult Review*, August, 1924 ; vol. xl, No. 2, pp. 102–8.
[85] Huw Lloyd, 1533–1620, who was apparently regarded as possessed of extraordinary powers of exorcism. Parson Richard Dodge, who was vicar of Talland in Cornwall from 1713 until his death, aged 93, in January, 1746, enjoyed the same reputation. See Thomas Bond, *Historical Sketches of the Boroughs of East and West Looe*, 1823, pp. 154–5: " About a century since the Rev. Richard Dodge . . . had the reputation of being deeply skilled in the black art, and could raise ghosts, or send them into the Red Sea, at the nod of his head."
[86] London, 1882, p. 297.
[87] *The Occult Review*, June, 1921 ; vol. xxxiii, No. 6, pp. 352–9.
[88] Vol. i, p. 294.
[89] Edited by Edith F. Carey, London and Guernsey, 1903, pp. 230–2. For a witch as a white rabbit, pp. 360–1 ; sorcerers as hares, pp. 361–5. See also pp. 315–337, witchcraft trials.
[90] *Irische Texte*, ed. Whitley Stokes and Ernst Windisch, iii serie, 2 heft. Leipzig, 1897, p. 377 (No. 215).
[91] *The Irish Version of the Historia Britonum of Nennius*, ed. with a translation by James Henthorn Todd. Irish Archæological Society, 1848, pp. 204–5, and note.
[92] A collection of pieces in prose and verse compiled and transcribed about 1100 by Moelmuiri Mac Ceileachair. A facsimile of the MS. (sixty-seven large quarto pages) was published Dublin, 1870. See 54b and 36 sqq.
For the heathenism of these transformations see *Irische Texte*, Stokes and Windisch, iii serie, 1 heft, Leipzig, 1881. [Do chuphur in da muccado] : suithi n-genntlecta la cectar-de in da mucuith 7 nus delbdais in cech riet . . . the learning of gentilism which enabled them to shift into any shape (p. 235).
The Rev. Edward Davies, *Mythology and Rites of the British Druids*, 1809, does not mention this art of shape-shifting. Mr. Lewis Spence, *The Mysteries*

of *Britain*, 1928, also has no remark upon metamorphosis, but he refers to Sir J. G. Frazer's *The Golden Bough* (*Balder the Beautiful*, vol. ii, 1923, pp. 41–3— Mr. Lewis does not give the exact reference, which is this), where it is suggested that the men and animals burned to death at certain Celtic festivals were warlocks, and sorcerers disguised in brute form. This is, to say the least, extremely hypothetical, and in view of the evidence from the *Leabhar Na H-Uidhri* inadmissible.

[93] *Folk-Lore*, vol. v, No. 4, pp. 310–11. Kuno Meyer, The Irish Mirabilia.

[94] *Acta Sanctorum*, Martii tom. ii, Antwerpiae, 1668, pp. 517–592.

[95] *Tripartite Life*, ed. Whitley Stokes, Rolls Series, 1887 ; part i, p. 249 and note ; part ii, p. 271 and note.

[96] Ed. Robert Atkinson, Dublin, 1887, 140b : " The Conarian Race of Ireland and Scotland."

[97] London, 1843, vol. ii, pp. 103–7. The poem is from MS. Cotton. Titus, D. xxiv, fol. 74, vo.

[98] Ed. Todd, 1848, ut cit. sup., pp. 204–5.

[99] Ed. by the Rev. James F. Dimock, *Works*, vol. v, 1867, pp. 101–7, Rolls Series. The book of Giraldus appeared in 1188, and was dedicated to Henry II.

[100] The adventure with the wolf-man took place in 1182 or 1183.

[101] S. Natalis, Abbot, is honoured as the founder of monasticism in North Ireland. The son of Aengus, he was of the royal family of Munster, and lived in the sixth century. He is the Patron of Invernaile, Donegal, and Kinnawly. Feast 27th January.

[102] " A female werewolf (*ben tét i cuanricht*) was called *conel*." *Irische Texte*, Stokes and Windisch, iii serie, 2 heft. Leipzig, 1897, p. 421.

[103] Lucius III (Ubaldo Allucingoli), elected to the Chair of Peter, 1st September, 1181 ; died at Verona, 25th November, 1185.

[104] Camden, op. cit., *Ireland*, p. 83.

[105] Temple, *Works*, 2 vols., folio, London, 1720. Volume the First, part ii, *Miscellanea*, p. 244. There is an interesting allusion to werewolfery in Giles Rose's *The Theatre of the World : or, A Prospect of Humane Misery*, 1679, being a translation of Pierre Boaistuau's *de Théâtre du Monde*, Paris, 8vo, 1558 (and many subsequent editions). The passage (pp. 204–5) runs : " Others have fancied themselves to be transformed into a Wolf, and ceased not from running at Nights with the Wolves over the Mountains and desart places, following their howlings and gestures through all places in the Country, so greatly were they tormented with their Distempers, till the Sun had cast her Beams and Rayes upon the Earth : The *French* call this Distemper the *Loupos Garoux* ; but the Greeks call this sort of Sickness *Lycanthropeia* : A thing that need not seem strange, nor fabulous to any that has read the holy Scriptures, and in it the pitiful estate of *Nebuchadnezzar*, who was transformed into an Oxe, for the space of seven Years, to reduce him to the knowledge of his God, *Dan*. 4."

www.ingramcontent.com/pod-product-compliance
Ingram Content Group UK Ltd.
Pitfield, Milton Keynes, MK11 3LW, UK
UKHW041419180426
11947UKWH00007B/223